'Bishop treats a fearful subject with an extraordinary lightness of touch; her humour and her emotional wisdom make this a delightful and humane novel.'
The Times

'Warm and emotionally convincing . . . effortlessly graceful'
Sunday Times

'Bishop is a fine, [...] moral and philosophical [...] *Telegraph*

Also by Bernardine Bishop

Unexpected Lessons in Love
The Street

BERNARDINE BISHOP

HIDDEN
KNOWLEDGE

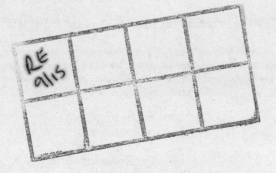

SCEPTRE

First published in Great Britain in 2014 by Sceptre
An imprint of Hodder & Stoughton
An Hachette UK company

First published in paperback in 2014

1

Copyright © The Estate of Bernardine Bishop 2014

The right of Bernardine Bishop to be identified as the Author of the Work
has been asserted by her in accordance with the Copyright, Designs
and Patents Act 1988.

A CIP catalogue record for this title is available from the British Library

ISBN 978 1 444 78927 0

Printed and bound by Clays Ltd, St Ives plc

Hodder & Stoughton policy is to use papers that are natural, renewable
and recyclable products and made from wood grown in sustainable forests.
The logging and manufacturing processes are expected to conform to the
environmental regulations of the country of origin.

Hodder & Stoughton Ltd
338 Euston Road
London NW1 3BH

www.hodder.co.uk

Chapter 1

It was the first anniversary of Betty Winterborne's husband's death. She sat down with a cup of coffee and looked out of the window. It was exactly the same view as she had looked at a year ago, the trees coming into leaf; the pigeons cheerfully flapping among the twigs; the houses opposite with the sun on them. This was the chair on which she had habitually sat after Jack's bed had been brought downstairs. She had sat here to chat with him, then to read to him, and then, in the final weeks, just to sit.

She was slightly irked that she must make a thing of the anniversary, and she didn't know what special thoughts or feelings to have. Close friends would remember to telephone; her daughter would probably feel she must mark the day somehow. But what was special about it? Now, however, sitting in the chair and looking out of the window, Betty felt she was getting an inkling. The branches of the tree were at exactly the same point, with regard to bud, leaf and pigeons, as they had been at the moment when she had heard Jack's first respiratory pause. 'Life must go on,' people had said to her a year ago. Why must it? What if it doesn't? But now she saw that it had. There was, after all, something to be said for an anniversary. Spring had come again. She was pleased to see it.

There was another less public anniversary, for it was at this time of year – not the day, exactly, but the season, and the general stage of the pigeons and the leaves – that, two years ago, Jack had been diagnosed. Betty and Jack had endured a year of the snakes and ladders that cancers and hospitals impose. Then, one year ago to the day, they had lost.

Betty was lonely. Loneliness must be differentiated from missing Jack. She did miss Jack. But the loneliness that gnawed her away was not the same as the missing of Jack, though it was easy to confuse the two, and, she felt, plenty of people might not bother to draw the distinction. Certainly, her friends did not do so, in their warm care of her widowhood. Only she knew that all her life, the fear of loneliness had been what moved her into action. She had married young, as she had intended to, for marriage and children were the insurance against loneliness. Not for her the hope that if she waited long enough she would find the unequivocal love another part of her longed to experience. She was a romantic, but she could not boldly live as a romantic, as some of her friends had continued to do into their late twenties, or, with hope dwindling, further. Jack was a good bet. He was tall and good-looking, had a First in Law, everyone liked him, and he was in love with her. Jack would do, and no one around her detected that what looked like romance was raw practicality. Jack had never known.

They had been happy. Jack had worked hard and was successful. Betty, who had read Modern Languages, pursued a more desultory career, featuring evening classes, tutoring and translations. She had not minded. She had liked being a help to Jack. She had taken pleasure in managing the social life his work generated. She had enjoyed keeping house. They had two children.

And all the time, for forty years, Betty had been one of a couple. The wolf of loneliness had not only been kept from the regularly painted front door of the North London Victorian terraced house in which Betty and Jack lived; the wolf had been forgotten. The fear of the wolf had been forgotten. The wolf had died, or turned into a fairy-tale, or a lapdog. Other frightening beasts had called, and one had ravaged her. But she had not known loneliness, or the terror of it. She had heard, without hearing, Jack's key in the lock at about seven every evening. Every day, she had planned, without planning, supper for two. She was aware, without rejoicing, of his presence in bed beside her. If there was time to watch a television programme, she would not watch it alone. If he was out, he was going to come home. If he was in, and both were working, one of them would soon, without noticing a motivation, go and find the other.

'I hate dying,' Jack had said. 'But I'm lucky, dying first.'

If Betty had died first, she thought, Jack would have missed her. He would have missed her, perhaps, more than she missed him. But it would have been different for him, because he did not have the predisposition to innate loneliness that for forty years had been secreting itself, unfelt but unaltered, deep inside her. He would have been lonely, but, once the worst of the missing had passed, he would not have been crippled by loneliness itself. And then, she thought, like many widowers, he would quite likely have replaced her.

For her, replacement would be difficult, even if any man were to look at a woman of sixty. Any antidote to loneliness depended on long-standing familiarity, depended as much on not having to have conversations as on being easily able to, as much on the known footsteps on the floor above as on being in the same room. This was why Betty's social life in the last year had not helped as much as friends had hoped it might.

However, another feeling had crept in gradually of late. This was a sense that her loneliness could, possibly, be met as a challenge, rather than suppressed as a malady. This was a new idea. She had never, in her quite long life, allowed herself to suffer her loneliness. She had evaded it. Perhaps to endure its darkness and coldness, instead of automatically switching on lights and turning up heating, was a necessary step for her towards maturity. She liked this thought. She did not want to die with her bogeys unfaced. Her grandfather had been killed on the Somme; her father had survived the D Day landings and never said a word about it. There was a toughness in Betty that she had never used. She had always been afraid it wasn't there. She hoped to be able to use it now, and she prayed it would be up to the job.

The telephone rang. It was Betty's daughter, Julia.

'Just remembering what day it is, Mum,' said Julia.

'Thank you.'

'How are you?'

'I'm fine.'

'What are you just doing? I've only got a moment, I'm between patients.'

'Having a cup of coffee. Being glad spring has come again.'

'Good. Are you doing anything this evening? I'll come over. With a bunch of flowers.'

'That's lovely. At about eight? We'll eat.' The problem of evening that day was solved, and as congenially as could be.

Betty thought about Julia. She was uneasy about Julia not being married, at thirty-eight. She used the word 'married' in her own mind, but if talking to a friend she would have said 'settled', to avoid seeming old-fashioned. Julia had been in two long relationships, but neither had ended in settledness. Conceivably, she had not wanted them to. Now past her first bloom, she was alone and childless. She threw herself into her work and was cheerful, and Betty saw no signs that her own loneliness was hereditary. But what a shame. That was the trouble these days. The women's movement seemed to have left the world even more a man's world than it was already. Betty thought that if she were young now she would not stand a chance of seeing how to cope. She admired Julia her hardihood.

~

'We must have a proper talk, tonight,' said Hereward Tree. He was speaking Italian. He looked steadily, his eyes intent and yearning, at Carina, beautiful, lively, and over thirty years his junior. She did not answer, but sat down beside him and took his hand.

He went on, 'Obviously I hope I will come through the operation alive and well. But it is a big operation, and I may not. You do realise that, don't you, darling?'

'I have looked it up on the internet. Usually people are all right.'

'Usually people may not have smoked quite as much as me.'

'No. But you are thin. That is important as well.' Carina shifted a little to be closer to him, and he smelt her scent. Whether he lived or whether he died, he thought, he had this moment.

'I love you,' said Hereward. It was a statement in which his whole life and self, at that stage of his life and self, were expressed. He hoped she realised she did not need to answer with a trite reciprocation. She said nothing, and looked at him tenderly. One of the wonderful things about her was that she understood when to let an utterance from his soul resonate and remain. After a moment's pause he went on. 'Tomorrow. Don't come and see me tomorrow. I shall be a mass of tubes and will not know whether you are there or not. Wait for Romola to tell you when to come.'

'I am afraid of Romola.'

'That doesn't matter. I know you are. In the next few days she will telephone and tell you when to come to the hospital. If all goes well I shall be home in a couple of weeks. We have a full time carer moving in. That is all arranged. You will not have to do anything for me. You will just sometimes let me look at you.'

'I will be afraid of the carer.'

'You'll get used to her.'

'I will want to do things to help.'

'OK, but you won't have to.'

'I shall cook meals.'

'OK, do that. Now, that is how it will probably be. But, on the other hand, I may die. If I do, Romola will inform you. I'm sorry about that.'

'But you will not die.'

'I hope not. In my will, I have left you all my money and this house, with everything in it. I have only left Romola the literary stuff. But now I want to give you a piece of very serious advice. If I die, I think you should go home to Genoa. You will have money, once the – ' Hereward did not know the Italian for the word probate, so said 'will', again – 'once the will is through. Later you will have a lot of money from the sale of this house and the

5

quite valuable things in it. Romola must organise the sale for you, and the money will be all yours.'

'I don't want to think about what if you die,' said Carina, who had, actually, been rather taken with the scenario.

'So now make love with me. Make love until morning. We haven't done that for a long time.'

'Yes, we will. But we will have supper first. Don't forget you aren't allowed to eat or drink after midnight. Anyway I am starving. So I will cook something now.'

Hereward was not hungry. He reluctantly let go of her hand and watched her hurry in the direction of the kitchen. Her back view was purposeful, and he smiled. Indeed he chuckled. After a minute he stood up, breathing heavily, leaning on a stick, and followed her. He could watch her cook. He did not want to miss a moment.

~

Roger Tree ran through the spring rain and encroaching dusk. His raincoat, heavy anyway, and with things in its pockets thumping his thighs, was now also wet. He arrived at his sister's front door and rang the bell.

Romola Tree had sat down to her marking. It used always to be a pile of exercise books, but now, of course, like everything else, it was typewritten and submitted in folders, which she found more difficult to transport than the exercise books had been. Nowadays she usually drove to and from the school where she worked. It was a short distance, and it would have done very well for the daily walk we are all advised to take, and she regretted forfeiting it. But, hard-worked and with an Ofsted looming, she could not take the time to think about her health. At fifty-five, she was at the height of her responsibilities, head both of her department and of a house. On her desk, as well as the pile of folders, were a cup of tea and a plate heavy with crispbread and cheese. She marked, sipped and nibbled; but she was not contented with her lot.

When the weekend came, she would sit at the same desk,

with no school folders and no plate. And she would get on with her novel.

It was her fourth novel, and its three predecessors had been turned down. She had an agent, but the agent was unenthusiastic, and the publishers, adamant. She persisted because it was what she enjoyed doing. She always had hopes, of course, as she did this time; and occasionally, when sleepless, made up her speech for the Booker Prize award night. Her first novel had been a fictionalised account of Wordsworth's relationship with Annette Vallon. The second had done much the same for Keats and Fanny Brawne. The next one was called *Withering Depths*, and had been a mistake, though still, at least in her own view, not without its subtleties. Now she was blissfully engaged on an ending for Mrs Gaskell's *Wives and Daughters*.

Because of her lack of success, she did not broadcast her novel-writing. But people who got to know her at all could not avoid realising it was her hobby and passion. Word went round. The headmistress had recently ribbed her about it. 'Like brother, like sister, eh?' she had said. Romola had not liked this. It was patronising. Her novels were not derivative of Hereward's. When Hereward and Romola were children, Romola, a year the younger, had been as inventive as Hereward. She had been as creative, and more literary. A mad wife had crept into their games, before Hereward had even heard of *Jane Eyre*. Romola's voice-overs belonged to the written word of Victorian novels, while Hereward's were colloquial, and, to Romola's mind, banal. It was Romola who wrote up in a succession of exercise books – she still had them – the stories that evolved from the antics of the job lot of dolls and toy animals laid out on the attic floor. Romola loved the game more than Hereward did. Sometimes she would say, 'Let's go upstairs for Hanulaland,' and he, for a minute, would look as if he would as soon be doing something else. But he had to come. He knew it was not a game you could play alone, and he knew you became absorbed, as in nothing else.

It was entirely their own. When Roger became able to climb the ladder to the attic, and his little face, smiling and triumphant, appeared suddenly one afternoon at floor level, Hereward and Romola stared at it with horror. 'You aren't allowed,' cried Romola, and at the same time, from Hereward, 'What are you doing here?'

A gentler version of that expression was on Romola's face now, when she saw who was on the doorstep, cowering from the rain. 'Roger!' she exclaimed.

'Can I come in?'

'Yes, come in. But I've got a pile of marking to do before tomorrow.' She helped him hang his raincoat, and took him into the sitting room, where, indeed, her marking was manifest. 'I suppose I know why you've come,' she said.

Roger looked astonished, then nervous. 'How could you know?'

'Hereward. Going into hospital tomorrow for his operation. You might be upset. But obviously that's got nothing to do with it.'

'Tomorrow? Is it? I had forgotten. I knew it was coming up, of course. Oh, dear – poor him. Triple heart bypass, isn't it?'

'Yes.' Romola didn't like to hear the operation called by its name, and disliked Roger for glibly so calling it, as if to compensate, by cheap medical lingo, for the fact that it had gone from his mind. For Romola, Hereward's state of health was a constant preoccupation. To hear the surgical procedure mentioned at this point jolted her into fresh spasms of anxiety. 'I'm sure he'll be all right,' she said, reassuring herself, as Roger did not require reassurance. 'Loads of people have them these days. The words make them sound worse than they are.' From having looked at a video of the operation on the internet, she knew this was not true.

'Well, why are you here, then?' she asked. She had still not offered him a drink. If he had a drink, she would probably have one, then she would have another, and then she would have lost her appetite for marking. Perhaps a cup of tea, but she could not be bothered.

'I wondered whether you could put me up.'

'Put you up? Why? Whatever's happened?'

'I can't explain. I suppose I should say that I don't want to explain. I'm sorry.'

'For heaven's sake! Have you lost your faith? Have you punched a parishioner? Have you run off with a parishioner's wife? Have you embezzled the collection boxes?'

But Roger was silent, staring at the floor. How could he smile at these sallies? He was unhappier than he had ever been in his life. Meanwhile his shoes were soaked, leaving traces on Romola's carpet, and he badly wanted a drink. 'None of the above,' he answered in a croaky voice.

'Tea, coffee or a drink?' said Romola, disconcerted to hear signs of tears. 'Have you had anything to eat?'

'Nothing to eat, thanks.'

She poured him a scotch, abstaining, so far, herself. She still hoped that the contours of her planned evening could be restored, but now she was becoming curious about Roger and what had brought him to her door. "You might as well tell me,' she said.

'OK.' He had drunk his scotch in two swallows, and his face seemed to Romola to be a better colour already. 'Can I have another?'

She responded by putting the bottle on a table at his elbow. He refilled his glass.

'I'm on bail,' he said. 'A young person I knew in my last parish has been to the police. He has said I sexually abused him. This is going back more than ten years. The police came, I was arrested, and suspended immediately from priestly duties. I can't stay in the presbytery. I could have, physically, but gossip was starting already. I have to disappear from the parish. I don't know where to go. I can't possibly stay in my presbytery. The bishop wasn't much help, though I know him, we were curates together years ago. This is absolutely dreadful. And all in a day, out of a clear blue sky.'

'And why is the young man making this accusation against you?'

Roger was silent. Then, for the first time that evening, he looked Romola in the eye. 'Because it's true,' he said.

There was a longer silence, a stunned one for Romola. She fetched another glass and poured herself a scotch. 'Not such a clear blue sky, then,' she said. Then she asked, 'Did you tell the police it was true?'

'Yes.'

Romola's face relaxed a little from its rictus of extreme censure. That admission must have taken some courage.

Roger went on, 'I couldn't make him – Tony is his name – feel disbelieved. It happened, and he is telling the truth. But why he has taken it into his head to come out with it ten – more like fifteen years later, of course I have no idea. We have corresponded about it in the past. I thought it was at rest.'

'At rest,' said Romola. 'Is that what the cover-ups are called? At rest!'

Hereward and Romola had never tried to understand Roger's conversion to the Catholic Church, nor his entering the priesthood. But they had treated these things with the greatest respect, joking about them, if at all, only with each other. Both of them had turned up for his baptism and for his ordination. Their mother had come with them, but their father was not persuadable. 'Did he but know it, he's only doing this to spite Dad,' whispered Romola to Hereward. 'Shhh,' said Hereward, who was liking the ceremonial. Hereward's sympathies were wider than Romola's, to her chagrin. She thought this was because he had a happier life.

'Hereward will have to know,' said Romola.

'I know. Everyone will have to know.'

'You poor thing.'

'I thought, being a novelist, Hereward might think something like "nihil humanum a me alienum puto".'

'Nonsense. It would be "alienum" to anyone except another paedophile.'

The word 'paedophile' stabbed Roger, rather as the phrase 'triple heart bypass' had Romola. But he bowed his head. What could he say? After a minute he repeated his earlier plea. 'Look, I'm awfully sorry, but can I stay with you? Probably not for very long.'

'Not for very long?' What he meant began to dawn on her. 'You're saying?'

'Yes. It'll be prison. Of course.'

~

Romola got up at five, hung over, to finish her marking. From the spare bedroom Roger heard her moving about quietly, probably trying not to disturb him. He had not slept, and so needed no such consideration. But he was grateful for it, and grateful that his sister had taken him in. He went over in his mind what he had to do – there was to be a committal, this morning, and various subsequent dates with police and probation, before his hearing came up.

He was intensely miserable. Around midnight he had closed the spare room door behind him, and his mind went back a couple of years, to the last time he had been in this room, in which his mother had lain dying, and had died. He knelt in prayer, leaning on a chair. He was not particularly tipsy, in spite of the whisky. Grief and fear seemed to have consumed the alcohol before his system had been able to. At this point he did not pray for forgiveness or for Tony; he had done that twelve years before. Now he prayed for courage. Then he did not pray for anything, but just prayed.

Then he took off a few clothes. His shoes and socks, and the bottoms of his trousers, were still soaking wet, so he arranged them on the radiator, which was tepid now, but perhaps would be warm by morning. He crept under the duvet. Hopkins's words, 'Creep, wretch, under a comfort, serves in a whirlwind', came into his mind. But in his case there was no comfort, however small, however derisory, to creep under.

If he could put his situation out of his mind, just for the time being, he would be able to sleep, and that would help him face tomorrow. But he could not put it out of his mind, for it was in his body. Even without specific thoughts, he was beset by the shivers and palpitations of fear, the dry mouth and the churning guts; and he was gripped by the heaviness and pressure of grief, an iron case drawn tight around his chest.

Lying as still as he could, sometimes too hot and sometimes too cold, he tried to think. In a fundamental way, his state was no different from what it had been twenty-four hours ago, when he had gone to bed thinking about the money for the church roof, whether he could stir his parishioners into concern over climate change, and, indeed, whether the diocese would approve solar panels, as the roof had to be done anyway. What luxurious worries these seemed now. That self was gone. It was gone for ever. There was this new self now, crying and sighing, throwing the duvet off and on again.

But fundamentally, there was no difference between yesterday evening and this. Yesterday, as much as today, he was the man who had committed the crimes he was accused of. Fundamentally, his crimes, and the harm he had done by them, were what mattered. The fact that he was now unmasked was trivial by comparison. This he told himself. But what grieved and terrified him in an immediate and physical sense was the fact that he had been found out.

He could feel with his conscience, though not with his body, that the facts that he would cease to be a priest in good standing, and that he would be sent to prison, were relatively trivial. He would suffer. That was just. He had not, after all, been a priest in good standing twenty-four hours ago. It was merely that people thought he was. But not everything that belonged to his good standing was trivial. He had been trusted by his parishioners, in his present parish, in the one before, and in the one before that. He had betrayed them. Twenty-four hours ago, he was already someone who had betrayed them. But twenty-four hours ago they did not know it. Now they did. He groaned in an agony that was far from trivial when he thought of Nora and Seamus, Xavier, Bernadette, Karol, Mbeke, Mrs Rafferty, and, oh, so many others, when they heard the news. Of course he would lose their love and respect, and he had loved their love and respect; but that belonged to the realm of triviality, and that loss to justice. What mattered was that they might lose faith in what he had tried to stand for, the hopes and aspirations whither he had tried to lead. And, of course, they would be without a parish priest, when priests are in short supply.

He got up and knelt at the chair again, to pray for his parishioners. If only it could be he that was the only one to suffer. But it could not be so. Suddenly he thought of, and prayed for, the mothers of the babies he had baptised. What would their feelings be? Let them keep faith with the Sacrament, he prayed, if not with its minister. He went back to bed, noticing that he reeked of sweat. In this next stage of the night he had another thought. Some of his parishioners would forgive him. It would take time. They would struggle inwardly; they would talk together; Damian or Maria might call a parish meeting. Many different views would be expressed. Many would pray for him. Some would say we are all human. Some would be too angry to say that, some too astounded to say anything. The bishop, Pip Jenkins, an old friend of Roger's, would have to make a formal visitation to the parish. Thinking of them forgiving him, perhaps lighting a candle for him, Roger sobbed.

Now it occurred to him for the first time that he could write a letter. Maria would see that it was read out at all the Masses one weekend. He would send it care of Maria. Sentences for the letter started to shape in his mind, and the letter began to serve as some sort of comfort in a whirlwind, for his wretched self to creep under.

Chapter 2

Julia Winterborne had recently moved flats. She had complicated feelings about the new purchase. It was on the small side, but in a more central location, and much more convenient for work. Her old flat, which she had bought five years before with financial help from her parents, got her feet on the property ladder, but had little else to recommend it. She never liked it. When her father died, he left her some money, to make death duties less of a problem later for Betty, to whom he left everything else. With this not inconsiderable sum, prudent Julia was able to move. She had a pleasanter environment, shorter journeys to the places she habitually went to, and her feet were planted several steps further up the property ladder. She was not able to love her new flat, which was in an ugly block, with an entry phone, and none of her windows looked out on to anything nice or leafy. But it was better than her first flat. When she next moved, she would have a more valuable asset to sell.

Her new flat had a startling lack of storage space, and Julia could not imagine how the previous people had managed. She still had stacks of boxes which could not be unpacked. This was not her way, her way being neatness, efficiency and despatch; but there was nothing she could do until she had spaces in which to put things away. This raised the question of whether to buy ready-made cupboards and bookshelves, or to build them in. She was tempted to measure up and to buy everything off the internet, in an evening; but a friend, illustrating the argument with her own flat, in which Julia was having supper at the time, showed how much more economic of space it was to build in storage spaces. The friend had a carpenter to recommend, the carpenter who had done the neat job Julia was admiring. Thus it was that Tony Tremlow rang Julia's doorbell by appointment one late afternoon.

Julia saw a thin, smiling, boyish man, probably in his late twenties, with plenty of curly hair, and a carpenter's bag on his shoulder. Tony saw a fair, trim woman, possibly about forty, who did not respond with more than a flicker to his smile, and immediately led him to the rooms where he would be working. No thought of a cup of tea, he noted. She was itching to explain exactly what she wanted, and this she did. However, she was soon pleasantly surprised, and sometimes silenced, by Tony's response. He was quick to see what was needed and what he could do, and had a few space-saving ideas of his own that Julia had not thought of. Her smile became unreserved. He was an ally, and they were a team. She made tea.

This was the first time they met. The second was a Saturday, and he came in his van, with a preliminary instalment of pale and beautiful wood. He came on time. Julia was impressed. She made tea at once, and they chatted while they drank it, mostly about the carpentry he was about to do, but about a few other things as well. He asked her what she did, and she said she was a dermatologist, and mentioned the hospital where she worked. He referred to a partner, and made no difficulties about revealing him as male. Then he began to work. Although Julia was out to lunch that day, and had plenty to do in the rooms that were not impossibly full of noise, she put her head many times round that door, and liked what she was beginning to see. The taking shape of her cupboards was remarkably quick, yet there was a lot to do. Julia was delighted at how impeccably Tony tidied up at the end of a working session. Hoover, broom, dustpan-and-brush were all enlisted. There would be quite a few evenings and a number more Saturdays before the job was finished. Julia did not mind waiting, if she could feel an end was in sight. A friend who knew about such things came round when Tony was not there, looked carefully and said Tony was a good carpenter. Julia telephoned the friend who had recommended him and was grateful.

Of course she wished he could come all day and every day until the job was finished. But he worked for a firm, and what he did for Julia he was doing in his spare time. She applauded his industriousness, and did not in the least mind paying him in cash.

One evening, over their now regular cup of tea, Tony was rather silent.

'Anything the matter?' asked Julia. She knew him well enough now to say that.

Tony made a determined face and pulled up the sleeve of his sweater well above the elbow. Julia had a definite impression of a muscled arm, and of golden hairs. 'Can I show you something?' he said. Julia said nothing, for she did not know what to expect. He pulled the sleeve up a bit higher, and said, 'Is this anything?'

She realised this was a medical question, and stood up. She took his arm in her hands. She was looking at a large mole with an irregular edge on Tony's shapely shoulder. She saw the artery in his neck beating fast. He was very anxious.

'It's OK,' she said. 'That's a dyplastic nevus. Rather large, but perfectly healthy.'

She felt his body relax. He breathed out. 'May I hug you?' he said, and did. 'I'm just so grateful.'

'Did you think it was melanoma?' she asked, pleased and slightly pink.

'Yes. I googled it, there were pictures, and it was obviously melanoma.'

'So why didn't you go to your GP?'

'Didn't dare. And what if he'd referred me to the hospital? I'd have been terrified.'

Julia could not deny that many GPs referred dyplastic nevi to Dermatology, and she herself looked at them in the hospital almost daily.

'Should I have it removed?' he asked. 'Before it turns into melanoma?'

She took his mole between her hands again, and ran a finger over its surface. She said, 'It's most unlikely to turn nasty. Obviously, in the remote possibility of its doing so, you'll take it to the GP.'

'How will I know if it "turns nasty"?' he used her expression with horrified fascination.

'Bleeds, itches, changes dramatically. But don't worry, it won't. Very few of them do.'

Julia was at her best, emotionally, when working. Patients, and at this moment Tony was a patient, saw a gentle, empathic, humorous side of Julia. Those closer to her experienced this seldom. Few patients went as far as to hug her, but many had been moved by her capacity to reassure. She had enjoyed being hugged by Tony.

That was the beginning of their intimacy. In the weeks that followed, Julia sometimes offered Tony a bite as well as tea when he arrived. Sometimes, if they got talking, she would watch him work, sitting on the bottom rung of a step ladder, or on a pile of planks that had not yet taken their destined places, and they would continue their conversation.

Once when this was happening, Tony said, 'Can I tell you something?'

'Yes.'

'When I was fourteen I was abused. Sexually abused.'

'Oh, dear.'

'It was a priest. Can I tell you about it?'

'Of course you can.'

Tony was silent, carefully aligning pieces of wood. When he had finished he went on, 'We were supposed to be Catholics, my family, but we weren't religious. I went to the ordinary comprehensive, not the Catholic school. The parish ran a Sunday School for Catholic children in non-Catholic schools. The class was taken by Father Rog. He really knew how to make religion interesting. I looked forward to the classes. Then he ran a reading group as well. It was wonderful. We started with *The Catcher in the Rye*; then we read loads of books – *The Black Arrow, Silas*

Marner, to name but a few, *Brighton Rock*.' He stopped again, and used the spirit level. 'Then there was an evening when he'd had a few drinks, there had been a parish get-together. He took me to his room to look at a novel by his brother, a famous author, to see if I thought it would be suitable for the reading group. That's when it started.'

'Good Lord,' said Julia. 'How awful.'

'It was awful, but exciting as well as awful. I felt special.'

'I suppose so, but how awful.' Julia wasn't sure she felt equal to being told this.

'Well, this went on for a few months, meeting secretly. Then he suddenly said we both had to go to Confession, and he was going to ask for a transfer to a different parish. That was the first he'd said about it being wrong.'

'But he must have known it was wrong.'

'I guess so. But he kept on saying things like it was love and all love came from God. I believed him. After all, he was a priest. Anyway, then he left. I haven't seen him since.'

'How awful,' said poor Julia again, lost for words. 'Did you tell anyone?'

'No. I haven't told anyone until recently. Now I'm telling everyone. I've been seeing a therapist for a year, gay man, very good. I talked about Father Rog lots. Much more than I expected. Anyway, I've been to the police. My therapist didn't tell me to, or anything. They don't, of course. But I know he thinks it's a good idea. Closure, maybe.'

'Yes. And to stop the priest abusing.'

'Yes. But now I've told the police, I'm telling everyone. My parents. My sisters. Friends. You. Once you start talking about it, you can't stop. I've become a clerical abuse bore. I like people being shocked.'

'Of course people are shocked.'

'Are you?'

'Of course. Awful for you keeping it bottled up all those years.' Julia wished she could stop using the word 'awful'.

'But now he'll be punished. He'll go to prison, you know.'

'As he deserves.'

'Yes. But it's a big thing, to make such a difference to someone's life. He probably hates me.'

'He may wonder why you left it so long.'

'Yes. I wonder, too. But there's such a lot about clerical abuse in the papers, in the news, nowadays. I thought, well, that happened to me as well. A bit of a band wagon, maybe.'

'So before now, are you saying you didn't really think about it?'

'I knew about it, and I think it made a difference to my life, my development, but I didn't think about it. You try to forget it, you know.'

'Well, Tony, I'm ever so sorry. I'm glad you've got a therapist.' When Tony mentioned development, Julia wondered if he would be straight without this awful seduction.

'Thanks. Thanks for listening. Have you thought you might like a hot air cupboard built above the hot water cylinder? Could be an airing cupboard. Airing clothes, keeping bedding. Would you like that? When I was a kid, the cat was always getting into ours, and you'd find him fast asleep among the towels.'

So the subject changed.

~

As soon as school was over for the day, Romola hurried to the hospital. She took the tube, which meant she would have to go home via school to pick up her car; but that was better than having to worry about parking in an unfamiliar quarter of London. She knew that Hereward would be in intensive care for a few days after his operation, but had understood that she would be allowed to see him. She found the huge hospital building confusing, but eventually arrived in an area which seemed to be right.

'I've come to see Hereward Tree,' she said to a woman behind a desk. 'I am his sister.'

The young woman consulted her computer. Then she consulted some papers in front of her. 'Mr Bleaney wants to see you,' she said.

'Mr Bleaney?' Romola was astonished, and could only think of an exceptionally bleak poem of that name by Philip Larkin.

'Hereward's surgeon, Mr Bleaney, wants to see you. He's put a note here.'

'Oh, he's a doctor. I see. Can't I see Hereward while I wait?'

'Not just yet.' A waiting area was indicated to Romola.

If Mr Bleaney wanted to see Romola, he was remarkably abstemious about that desire. She sat for a good half hour, amongst a few other disappointed and anxious relatives, reading the day's *Metro* and an ancient *Vogue*. Was this normal procedure, or did it betoken that something was wrong? What if Hereward was dead? Was this how hospitals broke such news to next of kin? Romola had no idea. Her mother had dealt with the nuts and bolts of her father's death, and, many years later, her mother died without recourse to hospital. Hospital culture was new to Romola. After half an hour she went back to the desk.

'Is Mr Bleaney on his way?' she asked.

Computer again. 'Bear with me. He's held up. He'll be here soon. Take a seat.'

Eventually a figure appeared in the waiting area, and said, 'Miss Tree?' The figure was in what Romola recognised from hospital dramas as the gear of the operating theatre. 'Can you just come in here?'

They went into a small room and he closed the door. 'Excuse me,' said Mr Bleaney, 'I haven't changed out of work clothes, as you see. I hurried to meet you as soon as I heard you were here. Well, how do you do? I'm Mr Bleaney. I operated on your brother this morning. The operation went well. Post-operatively, in recovery, something rather unexpected happened, I'm afraid. Your brother underwent a massive cerebrovascular accident. It is something that happens, but rarely.'

'So – do you mean he hasn't come round?'

'No, he hasn't come round.' Mr Bleaney spoke kindly and quietly, using Romola's language, when another would have come more naturally to him.

Tears of shock and grief were finding their way down Romola's cheeks – she who never cried. 'Is this a stroke?'

'Yes.'

'A bad one?'

'Yes.'

'Will he come round?'

Mr Bleaney was silent. Then he said, 'In surgery we never say never. But if your brother does regain consciousness –' to colleagues he would put this process in different words – 'he will be severely brain-damaged. Very severely. We know enough already to be sure of that. I am very sorry.'

'Then he should never have had the operation,' cried desperate Romola.

'I'm going to ask someone to bring you a cup of tea. This has been a bad shock for you. The operation was indicated, because of the condition of his heart, and there were no risk factors except the smoking. These things happen, and we are very sorry when they do.'

'Can I see him?' Her voice was a child's.

'We suggest not today. Wait until we get him a ward, or possibly a room. Remember, if you saw him, he would not know you were there. Best is, if you ring the hospital in a day or two and they will tell you when he is out of intensive care. Then we can review the situation and the picture will be clearer. That is a better time for you to see him. I have to go now; I am still in theatre. I will get someone to bring you a cup of tea.' He looked at her. 'Or a brandy.'

'Neither, I'm going home.'

Mr Bleaney scrutinised her as she stood up. Was she the type to sue? Not that she would have a case. He was genuinely sorry this had happened to Hereward Tree, of whose books Mrs Bleaney was a fan. But the operation had been perfect. Students had looked on; everyone had been impressed. Mr Bleaney was a very good heart surgeon. Perhaps he shouldn't have used the word 'accident' to Miss Tree. People sometimes misunderstood that term. But it was too late to correct any false impression – she had gone. Clearly it hadn't occurred to her that it was a privilege to be given the bad news by him in person. He sighed and went back to theatre.

~

Romola took taxis almost as seldom as she cried, but she took one now, and stared out of the window, seeing nothing. What had happened to Hereward was more terrible than death. She had contemplated his death before the operation, though only because if you envisage something, it makes it less likely to happen. But she had never thought of this. He too had contemplated his death, and talked it over with her; but this particular eventuality he had not imagined. The loss of Hereward's mind, without the loss of the whole of him, emphasised for Romola, in an extraordinary way, the loss of Hereward. There he was, somewhere in that hospital, his body a mass of tubes and machines. But his thoughts, memories, feelings, perceptions, were nowhere. Throughout Romola's life, Hereward had been there. Romola had not known a world without Hereward. Hereward was always interested, and never afraid. That was his approach to life. He was stimulated, not cowed, by disasters. Events, even the most perilous ones, were always adventures, rather than dangers. Sailing with Hereward, they had got into rough waters, but she had never been frightened, because he was not frightened. Once she was nearly frightened, until he said, 'Have you forgotten? You are always safe with Hereward.' Now, without Hereward, Romola was not safe. A hurricane of outer air could reach her now. It was reaching her. How, at this late stage, could she learn her own way of being safe, when she had always sheltered in him?

But what about him? This is not about you, she told herself. It was Hereward's tragedy, not her tragedy. At the age of fifty-six, at the height of his powers, happy in a new relationship, he had been mysteriously extinguished. This was a disaster that was not going to bring that familiar look of intrigued concentration to his face.

Then Romola realised she did not believe Mr Bleaney.

Hereward would recover. He might recover slowly. Perhaps he would even recover suddenly. Mr Bleaney might know Hereward's insides, but he did not know Hereward. He thought he knew his heart, but he did not. Hereward would come through this, as he had come through his losses in love, the plane crash, his reversals of fortune, his heart attacks. She might have a message on the telephone when she got home. ' You might have heard I've had a mishap, but all is well.'

She cried and paid the taxi driver.

'Cheer up,' he said. 'It may never happen.'

'It has,' she said. She went into the house, and remembered she should have gone back to school for her car. How long ago that little piece of planning seemed now. Then she heard Hereward's voice call from the sitting room. 'Romola?' It must be the answerphone. She gasped with joy. It was not until this moment that she remembered Roger was staying with her, and realised that the voice she had heard was his.

'I've cooked some supper,' said poor Roger proudly, coming to the door to find her. 'Lamb chops, baked potatoes and broccoli. All ready. Whatever's the matter?'

'Hereward,' said Romola.

'Not dead?' Roger took her elbows in his hands, incommoded by a spatula. 'Dead?'

'Stroke. Brain damage. Unbelievable.'

However, they did sit and eat. Roger had laid the table. He had picked a flower from the front garden, and put it in a vase in front of Romola's place. He had envisaged quite a different homecoming for her from her long day's work and her hospital visit. 'Did you see him?'

'No, I wasn't allowed to.'

After supper, Romola said, 'Oh Lord, I forgot, I have to ring Carina. Rog, I can't. Will you? She's not scared of you.'

~

It was a few days later that Julia next spent an evening with Betty, her arrival this time unaccompanied by flowers. The flowers lived on, however, in a vase in the sitting room. There sat Julia and Betty, having eaten rather an unsatisfactory supper. Betty had lost interest in cooking, though she made more effort for Julia than otherwise.

Julia felt a certain disquiet about Betty, a disquiet not purely unselfish. Betty was her responsibility, now that Dad was dead. She did not quite like the way Betty said, 'Now it's just the two of us'. She did not like the way Betty had once said, when Julia was complaining about money, 'You could always move in here, darling. It would be much cheaper for you than paying the mortgage on your flat'. Julia had not complained to Betty about money again.

Julia's trouble was she could not help feeling attracted to living in the house of her childhood, taking her old bedroom back, or perhaps taking Mark's bedroom, which was bigger. She loved this house, with its big garden. Her flat was all very well, and its cupboards and shelves made it more tolerable, but Julia did not really like flats. And yes, of course it would be cheaper. The size of Julia's new mortgage depressed her. Those were motives. But there was another motive as well, and this was the one that made Julia suspicious of herself. It would be a voluntary return to her childhood and adolescence. She would have given up trying to build her own life. Her mother, not a man, would be her companion and housemate. The trouble was, it would be perfectly bearable. It would be effort-free. Together they would make decisions about redecoration and a new cooker. Perhaps Tony would build them an airing cupboard. They would have their television programmes, and their jokes. Julia knew she could settle to becoming the spinster daughter, and this is what she feared. The role would not be imposed on her. She would slide into it. Indeed it was not a role; it was a part of herself. As a grown up woman, she felt a failure. There was a lure, a siren-song, about the notion of cutting her emotional losses and moving back into the parental home. She had taken all this to her therapist, of course, and it had been well canvassed. Perhaps she was identifying with her father, and trying to take his place. Perhaps she wanted to turn the tables on her mother, and, as her mother got older, be the one with the power. Or perhaps Mark came into the picture somewhere.

A few centuries ago, it would have been a perfectly normal thing to do. The daughter lived with the widowed, ageing mother, presided over the mother's death, and inherited the house. In this century, Julia would be looked at askance; she would be seen as unfledged.

More than anything, Julia wanted a baby. This was another reason to be hostile to her new flat, up lots of stairs, and small. Fine for a single dermatologist; no good for a mother and baby. The baby problem had recently come to outweigh career considerations, in her imagination and sense of her future. She dated this change of focus to the break-up of her relationship with Stan. She was thirty-eight. Neither of her long-term partners had led to a baby. Stan, the man with whom she had the more serious relationship, already had children, and did not want another. With his predecessor, Julia had become pregnant. Calling on her usual decisiveness, she had gone for an abortion at an early stage, and alone. She had not told Jack and Betty. As she walked across the square to the clinic, she saw three women with placards standing in the drizzle. One placard said, 'Are you sure you won't regret destroying your baby?' and another, 'You may not get another chance'. She responded with acute recognition to both sentiments now; but at the time they were only annoying, and, if she could have been bothered, she would have complained. She did regret her abortion, and she did fear, now, that she would not get another chance; and she sometimes would find herself daydreaming about how she might, indeed, contrary to her conviction at that time, have managed a baby, with maternity leave from her medical training. Pat would have been a hopeless father, but Pat would not have stayed. Pat would not have mattered. The baby would now be twelve. Julia had decided at which local secondary school he would just have started. Or she.

The important thing was to have a baby now, and quickly. Her relationship with the amply be-childed Stan had finished over a year ago, almost certainly because he was unsympathetic about

Jack's illness. She had thrown Stan out, and now he was with someone else. It would be ignoble to ask him for a one-night stand, which might extend to several nights: her fertility would not be what it was. But what if she asked him for a modicum of sperm? She had loved him once, and would like him to be the father of her child. A rather desperate alternative was the internet, from which she knew sperm could be acquired.

Julia was fond of Betty, and had always, basically, got on well with her. Betty had not been a difficult mother. She and Jack had been a good couple to grow up with. They loved each other and loved their children. They were neither cold nor excessively involved. They were wonderful about Mark, considering. If Jack were the one widowed in the big house, and Julia pregnant, Julia would have been happy to move in with him. If Julia and her pregnancy were to move in with Betty, it would solve the same problems, indeed solve more in relation to child-care; but it would create others. Would she come to hate Betty, standing for, as she would, and colluding with, Julia's lack of a man in her life? They would be like a family of elephants, grandmother, mother, and calf. Thinking of this, Julia laughed, but humourlessly. Then she had a cheering thought. There was no reason to suppose that she would never again meet a man she could love. The elephant family need not be a life sentence.

Actually, Betty did not entertain private hopes that Julia would move in with her. If Julia had made the suggestion, Betty would not have been able to prevent herself from welcoming it, open-armed, smiling with joy. It would have afforded a respectable reprieve from taking on her struggle with loneliness, and would have transformed her weakness, seamlessly, into parental complaisance. But such a development would have surprised her. She was much more confident than was Julia herself that Julia had a life of her own. Betty did not see Julia as unfulfilled, in spite of the regrettable absence of husband and children. Betty's version of Julia was that she was too hard working and too successful professionally to mind intensely about a personal life. She admired Julia for this. It was so unlike herself.

After Julia left, Betty slipped quickly into loneliness. Instead of hurrying off to bed, she sat down and tried to look loneliness in the eye. Was it akin to boredom? Akin to fear? To homesickness? To being unwanted? Excluded? What was the nature of it? Was it, really, anything to be afraid of? Perhaps the means she was accustomed to take to avoid it – daytime television, wandering round Sainsburys with a trolley, lunching with uninteresting acquaintances – rather than the loneliness itself, were what sapped her morale. Perhaps the side effects of the treatment were worse than the illness. This was an interesting possibility. She wished she could tell Jack these new thoughts, but, of course, he had never known about the loneliness; nor, during those years, had she.

Chapter 3

Carina was very sad, and Roger had taken to walking round to Hereward's house to visit her. Roger it was, of course, who had broken the news to her. She had been bewildered and had cried. She called Roger 'Padre', which he didn't think was correct, because he was not a member of a religious order. In no other sense did he deserve it, either; but he had not told Carina that.

'Padre,' she said. 'Have you seen Hereward yet?' They spoke English.

'No. Romola has.'

'What did she say?'

'Well, he is just lying there.'

'In hospital bed?'

'Yes. With machines all around him.'

'Unconscious?'

'Yes.'

'He may get better. Are you praying for him?'

'Yes,' said Roger, who had done so only in a formal and cursory way. His worries about his own life ousted other prayers. To Carina, he could see, there was no reason why a brother's sudden vegetative state was not a constant preoccupation for a brother. 'Have you any brothers, Carina?'

'Two, and one sister. They are in Genoa. They think I am living a bad life, and so do my parents. Do you think so, Padre?'

'No.'

'Hereward said if he died I should go home to Genoa. He has not died. But how long will he be unconscious?'

'No one knows. They think perhaps always.'

'Then what should I do, Padre?'

'I don't know. But I'll think about it.'

'I am afraid here, without Hereward. I have never slept in a house alone. There are noises in the night. I was never afraid, with Hereward.'

'I'm sorry.'

'Also I have no money. I eat what is already in the fridge and the freezer.'

'Well I'm sure we can sort that out.'

'Should I go and see Hereward?'

'Yes, why not?'

'Will you come with me, Padre?'

~

Roger called for Carina the next afternoon, and they went to the hospital. Hereward was now in a small room off a cardiac ward. He lay quite still, with his eyes closed. Tubes went into his nose, and, under the neat, cellular blanket, were finding ways to other, unknown parts of his body. Machines flashed and pulsated. A nurse, doing something nearby, registered the visitors' arrival. 'I am his brother,' said Roger.

Hereward's hands were folded on the white blanket. They looked like the hands of a peaceful person to Carina, and to Roger, who had seen a lot of death, like those of a dead person.

'He looks only asleep!' said Carina. She sat on the chair beside the bed while Roger stood. She touched one of Hereward's hands. 'Hereward,' she said. 'Hereward. *Ecco* Carina.' She turned to Roger. 'His hand is warm.'

Hereward lay like a statue. Much though he would have loved to see Carina, he could not. Carina picked up one of his hands, and called him again. Well, thought Roger, looking at the hand, chafed by Carina's little ones, whatever cleaning up they have done of him, they have not got the nicotine stains off.

Carina called Hereward again, more urgently. Attracted by a raised voice, the nurse came near, and said, 'It's no good, darling, he won't hear you.'

'But does he know I am here?'

'I'm afraid he doesn't. I'm sorry. Are you his daughter?'

'A friend,' said Roger.

The nurse's interest in Carina's distress dwindled. She looked at Roger. 'You know he is in deep coma, don't you,' she said quietly to him.

'Yes. We know that. My sister has told us.'

'Oh yes, we know Romola very well. I am so sorry. It's a terrible thing for a family. You are suffering more than he is.'

'Maybe,' said Roger, as the nurse receded. 'Maybe.'

~

Tony Tremlow was running out of people to tell his story to. Then he remembered Gerry, who had been at school with him, and had been a member of the parish Sunday school. Tony would get a rapt audience there. He rang the most recent number he had for Gerry. Gerry answered.

'Hi, it's Tony, Tony Tremlow.'

'Oh, hi. Long time no—'

'Have you got a minute?'

Gerry had. Tony gave him a shortened version of the story, complete in essentials. He could tell that Gerry was riveted. He was unprepared for Gerry's response.

'You jammy bastard!' said Gerry. 'You know you can get compensation for that.'

Suddenly Tony did not want to continue the conversation. It was interest, shock and sympathy he liked, certainly not this. Soon he found a reason to ring off.

The next day, however, Gerry rang him. 'You know what you were telling me yesterday?'

'Yes.'

'That was Father Rog. But there was also a Father Pip. Do you remember?'

'Yes, of course I do.'

'He took me for maths coaching.'

'I remember that.'

'He used to touch me up, the dirty bugger.'

Tony had a strong hunch this was untrue. Talk about a band wagon. This was possibly a financial band wagon. 'Look, are you sure?'

'Course I'm sure. I've decided to go to the police. It'll be my word against his.'

'So you expect him to deny it.'

'Of course he will. But they believe the victim.'

'It's a very serious thing, you know.'

'Was serious for me. You should know that yourself.'

'Father Pip's a bishop, now.'

The wind was taken out of Gerry's sails by this information, but a fresh gust quickly blew in. 'All the worse,' he said, after half a minute.

'Father Rog didn't deny it,' Tony said.

Again, Gerry's sails sagged, but picked up. 'They mostly deny it,' he said. 'My bastard probably will.' Obviously his course was set.

They rang off, Tony regretting he had made contact with Gerry. That was the last time he sought to tell his story just for the fun of it. He felt terrible, and looked forward to his next session with his therapist, when he could get his terrible feeling off his chest.

~

A few days later, Bishop Philip Jenkins got Roger on the phone. Roger was touched, assuming Pip wanted to support him; but that was not the purpose of the conversation. Pip was evidently harassed and upset.

'Rog. Have you heard anything?'

'From the police? Only my next bail appointment.'

'No, about me. Well, clearly you haven't. Do you remember that boy Gerard Farrell, at St Thorlac's?'

'Yes.'

'He's been to the police to say I molested him. I've had to disappear. It's been put about that I'm having a breakdown from overwork. The police came.'

'So where are you now?'

'The nuns at St Fabian's have taken me in. Sister Scholastica believes I'm having a breakdown. But it'll all come out. The police have been questioning me. I'm on bail.'

Roger could not help his first feeling being a physical rush of pleasure that someone else was in the same boat as him. He hid this, and Pip did not seem to suspect it. 'What has Gerry Farrell actually said?' Roger asked.

'I don't know if you remember I used to take him for maths coaching. It sounds so suspicious put like that, doesn't it? But it was maths coaching and nothing else. There is no truth in this accusation.'

'Of course not,' said Roger. 'All that time you were madly in love with Gina McGee, a respectable mother of three. I remember it all.'

'Good. That might help. But because of you, they will say there was a culture of abuse at St Thorlac's at that time. What am I going to do? I am stunned. There is no shred of truth in it. Why should someone make it up?'

'Money,' said Roger. 'Compensation.'

Pip was silent. Then he said, 'But you actually did yours, didn't you?'

'Yes, and I admitted it to the police. And to you, as my bishop.'

'Had you ever done it before?'

This was something Roger never spoke about, but now he said, 'Yes, in my first parish.'

'Did you tell the police?'

'No. It never came out and never will. I've never told anyone before, by the way, except in confession, so confidentiality, please.'

'I shan't probe,' said the bishop. His mind turned back to himself, and the present. 'But what if one hasn't done it? I don't feel I've got a leg to stand on. The police obviously didn't believe me.'

'Where did you see Gerry, for the lessons?'

'Well, that's the awful thing. In my room. Nowhere in the

presbytery was free the night I used to see him. You know how cramped we were there, with all the initiatives we had on the go. So I took him up to my room. One thought nothing of it, in those days. Or I didn't. Nothing could have been more chaste. But I can't prove that. It's his word against mine, and he's the one who will be believed. Who already is believed.' Roger heard Pip start to cry.

'It's much worse for you than for me,' said Roger, 'because I did it. For me it's justice.'

'Not for me it ain't,' said the bishop. He blew his nose.

'I can speak up for you,' said Roger. 'I'll tell them about Gina McGee. Perhaps we could get her as a witness.'

'She never knew I loved her.'

There was a silence. Then Roger said, 'Thank God Michael is dead.' Michael was the saintly parish priest of St Thorlac's with whom Roger and Philip had worked.

'He must be turning in his grave.'

~

Romola went to Hereward's house and let herself in with her key. She called 'Hello?' so as not to give Carina a fright. But Carina did not appear to be in.

It was a Saturday, and by rights Romola should have been thinking about Molly Gibson and Cynthia Henderson, née Kirkpatrick; but all thoughts of her novel had, for the moment, been driven from her mind. Before she set forth this morning, she had carefully re-read the instructions received from Hereward before he went into hospital. They were not on email, nor typed. He had written them in his familiar hand.

Darling Romola,

INSTRUCTIONS
If I live:
> *Come and see me in hospital. Check if Carina wants to come, and if she does, bring her. Don't persuade her to.*

A full time carer is moving in when I get home. Ring Care-Angels, 7532 6800, when you get word of my release, and activate them. They are expecting that. Make sure the carer is in situ BEFORE I arrive home. Try to be here yourself.

If I die:
As you know, I have left the house, its contents, and any current moneys to Carina. You will have to help her sell the house. Or possibly her Dad, who is a businessman, will take charge. I think she should go home to Genoa, and she will be rich. If she meets someone else and decides to stay in London, that's fine. They can live in the house if they so wish, obviously. It will be her house.

That's all as it turns out. The important thing is to make sure she has enough immediate money, which you can reclaim from her legacy when the probate comes through. My solicitors you know.

You should ring Care-Angels, to say they won't be wanted.

You are the executor of my will, of course, with Rog, who won't be needed to do anything, but you have to have two.

You inherit my literary estate and any moneys forthcoming. This looks pretty good at the moment. They are making a film of No Holds Barred, *as you know. I am so glad to be able to make you comfortable, and if I die, that will be a (small) consolation for each of us.*

There's a stack of my books in typescript – all of them, I think – on the floor in my study, under the window. On the top of the stack is the book I have been writing for the last six months, which is not quite finished. It is near enough finished, though. I will work on it if I live, but as it is, it exists. It's also in my computer, under documents, title Current Novel. *Send it to my publisher.*

In fact I am now sending it to your computer, for safe-keeping. There, Sent. Please make sure it is dedicated to Carina. That is the most important thing. She can tell you her surname, and spell it for you.

So Romola knew what to do if Hereward lived, and if he died. What she did not know was what he would want her to do in the situation that had arisen, and that no one had foreseen. She rang Care-Angels, and said a carer should be put on hold. Care would probably be needed, but would not be needed yet. Romola could not bear to say care would never be needed. Indeed if Romola's wrist had been strapped to a lie detector, at this stage it would have registered that Hereward would recover.

Roger had told her that Carina was worried about money. Romola had with her a hundred pounds in cash, held by a rubber band, which she now put on a table. It was Romola's own hard-earned money, and she found herself reluctant to give it to Carina. When would it be repaid, in the event of Hereward living on? But she had to give it to Carina for Hereward's sake. She had done some thinking about strategies to meet this problem. Hereward had possessions that could be sold, perhaps at auction. Not having ever thought about accumulating valuables herself, this was new to Romola. But she was aware that it could be done.

A great deal of money was needed. The hospital was of the view that Hereward would be better off in a specialist unit, probably because they wanted to clear his bed. Poor Hereward had become a bed-blocker. It would be a private specialist unit. It would cost the earth. Carina might never come into her fortune.

At this moment Romola heard a soft tread on the stairs, and the frightened face of Carina came round the door. She started when she saw Romola, but looked relieved. 'I heard someone and I did not know who it could be,' said Carina. 'I did not know anyone had a key except me and Hereward.'

'I've left you some cash on that table,' said Romola, thinking that, when all was said, Carina was certainly very beautiful. 'But we should raise a bit more money, so that you can be comfortable. Hereward would want that. Also you'll want to pay me back the hundred pounds I'm lending you.' She had visited Carina already to offer condolences, and did not feel called on to reaffirm them today.

'Yes,' said Carina. 'That's OK.'

A bit more than OK, I should have said, thought Romola. She went on, 'I think the best idea is to sell Hereward's collection of stones. That will do for a start. Some of them will fetch a lot of money.'

'I do not know where they are,' said Carina.

'No. But I do. I am going to take them with me now, and find the best way of selling them. It will be several thousand, perhaps very much more. I'm taking this on my own head.'

Not knowing this expression, Carina looked at Romola's head, to see if any stones were there. Carina had only just woken up. It was twelve o'clock, and she did not want Romola to know she had slept so late. But Romola did know.

'Do you agree?' said Romola. 'I'm going to put it in writing. You have a cup of coffee.'

Leaving Carina, Romola went into Hereward's study. She stood in the middle of the room and looked round her. She saw the crowded desk, the chair at an angle as if its occupant had that minute risen, the full ashtray. She smelt Hereward. She cried. Tears poured down her face, and she heard quiet moans forcing themselves through her throat. 'I don't know if I can bear this,' she said.

In a way Hereward was more present in his sunny study than he was in his bed in the hospital. She would go to the hospital later. When the nurses' backs were turned she always spoke to Hereward, held his hand and tried to wake him.

She approached the desk and took a piece of paper. She wrote *Financial Matters* at the top. She wrote the date, and that she had given Carina a hundred pounds. She then wrote that she was taking the stone collection to sell. She knew where to find the key of the cupboard in which Hereward kept his collections. She had a plastic carrier bag in the pocket of her jacket, and put the stones in that. She was careful, as she did not want them to scratch each other; but she did not wrap each in tissue paper as she should have. She did not have the heart. Nor the tissue paper. It would be the pictures, when all the collections had been sold, she thought. Hereward would not mind, as long as Carina was provided for. Carina could stick posters of pop stars on the patches of wall the pictures left behind. If that happened, and Hereward came safely home, he would laugh.

She would have to go with Carina and open a bank account for her. Or perhaps Roger could do that as he had nothing to do. Were priests allowed to open bank accounts? But then, was Roger still a priest? When the bank account was open, by whatever agency, Romola would be able to issue Carina with money regularly, from the proceeds of the valuables. There were rare books, Romola now remembered, as well as collections and pictures. There would be enough money at least to start Hereward in his new unit. The sale of Hereward's house, if necessary, would come later. That was a worry, for if Hereward recovered, and his house had been sold, where was he to live? But if Hereward recovered, nothing in the world would matter.

Then Romola went to the stack of typescripts under the window. They were very neat. In his own way, Hereward was well organised. Romola remembered how in the days of Hanulaland he always tidied up at the end of a game. His 'people', a gnome, two rabbits, three small teddies, a soldier, and sundry other shabby artefacts, which, with her similar lot, had been the inspiration and springboard for the stories, were always lined up in a row on a particular piece of carpet for tomorrow. He did the same with her 'people', on another piece of carpet. She watched, disapprovingly. She would have preferred to have the 'people' loose and muddled overnight, as if the game was still going on in the absence of its creators. But she had learned not to take issue with Hereward about things that did not really matter. The game mattered too much to risk putting him off it.

She had asked Hereward some years back why he kept his

novels in typescript long after they had been published. He raised an eyebrow at her, and answered, 'For you to offer to King's after I'm dead?'

'You can offer them to King's yourself. And why should you die first?'

'I'm older, male and a smoker. And I've got a heart. I'll be like Dad, popping off at seventy, you'll be like Mum.'

Romola was glad that their mother had died, peacefully, with her three children at her bedside, not having to know what was to happen to Hereward or what was to happen to Roger.

On the top of the stack of typescripts was the new novel, the one that had been regarded in Hereward's instructions either as finished or unfinished, which also existed as an unopened attachment in Romola's inbox. She made a further entry on her piece of paper: *Untitled manuscript novel taken home by Romola.* It seemed safer to have it under her own roof.

Chapter 4

Betty always leafed through the local paper when it arrived on her doormat. How did it make any money, she wondered, if it was free, and, presumably, had to pay people to deliver it? She found many things in modern life difficult to understand, but not usually because they were free. She put the newspaper on the kitchen table, and began to turn the pages, conferring on each no more than a glance.

But now something caught her eye. It caught her eye because she saw a name she knew. She began to read the paragraph carefully. Roger Tree, parish priest of Our Lady of Calvary, had been removed from office, after admitting to sexual assaults on a fourteen year old in 1997 in a previous parish. Roger Tree was now on bail and his hearing was pending.

Betty knew Roger Tree. Her scalp prickled with shock and horror. She stared. Then she went to the telephone and dialled Julia's number. Julia would be working, but would ring back when she was free.

'Will you ring me when you can?' was Betty's message.

She went back to the newspaper, and read the paragraph twice more. She had every reason to remember Father Roger Tree. He was the person who had tried and failed to save Mark's life. She and Jack had kept in touch with him for a while after Mark's death, and there had been a big Mass for Mark, said by Father Roger. Betty was not a fervent, nor even a practising Catholic, and Jack was not religious. But both had been pleased when they discovered that Betty's nominal Catholicism, and some attendance at Mass, could get Julia, and five years later, Mark, into the Catholic primary school, widely agreed to be the best of the local schools. It was academically the highest flying, which did not say much; and it was the best managed. The headmistress was impressive. In time Jack became a school governor. Its chaplain was Father Roger Tree, who was a curate at the church next door to the school. The church was St Malachy's, and the school was also of that name. Its bright blue and magenta uniform was well known in the neighbourhood.

The telephone rang and it was Julia. 'Yes?' she said, displeased to be forced to phone her mother in the middle of work.

'Do you remember Father Roger Tree?'

Julia was silent. The name was familiar, but she had not heard it for over twenty years.

So Betty went on. 'He was the chaplain at St Malachy's school. He was on the trip when Mark was drowned. He tried . . .'

'Of course I remember, now,' said Julia. 'He wasn't chaplain of St Malachy's in my day. He came after I left. But of course we knew him because of Mark.'

'He's in the local paper, darling. I can't believe it. Child abuse. He's admitted it. He's on bail. He's going to be tried.'

'My God, Mum.'

'I know.'

'I'll ring you later. Or shall I come over tonight?'

'Please do.'

'There's a bit of work I have to do. I'll come over after supper.'

Before the conversation was over, and even more so after it, Julia was struggling with her own private realisations. Tony Tremlow's 'Father Rog' must be one and the same as the attractive young priest who, she remembered, had come to talk to her parents when Mark died. Twenty years or more separated the two occasions when life had made Julia aware of Roger Tree's existence. She was undergoing, as well as shock, the strange pleasure that attends on events unexpectedly coming together. The coincidence, in itself, was enthralling. Julia calmed herself for her next two patients, read a colleague's paper while she ate her supper, and then set forth for her mother's.

~

Betty looked pale and untidy when she opened the door.

'You're shaken, Mum,' said Julia.

They sat down, quite close to each other, on two chairs in the sitting room, and Julia read the newspaper paragraph. She was relieved that Betty seemed to have the heating on, as it was evidence that Betty was looking after herself. At this moment Betty felt there was no one in the world except Julia that she had anything in common with. This worried her, but she had no time for this worry.

'We know he abused in 1997,' said Betty, speaking slowly, as she pondered. 'He knew Mark, it must have been, in the late eighties and up to 1990. I wonder when he arrived at St Malachy's? You say he wasn't chaplain when you were there. He must have arrived at St Malachy's some time between 1985, when you left, and a year or so before Mark died. I'm trying to remember when Mark started talking about him. I wish Jack were here. He might remember.'

'What are you thinking?'

'Whether . . .' Stricken, Betty stared at Julia.

'No, I don't think so,' said Julia. 'I really don't. The abused child here is fourteen. That's quite different from a nine, ten year old. Different pathology. This victim would have been in puberty. Mark certainly wasn't. Mark was little.'

'I know.'

'I see what you are worrying about. But I don't think you need.' Julia was not so sure, herself; but this was an anxiety she could not bear her mother to have. What could be done about it now?

'We never understood why he jumped,' said Betty.

'Yes, we did. He was very nimble, and he was a show-off.'

'There's something I've never told you. I've never told anybody, because it wasn't important. But now I don't know if it was important or not.'

'Tell me.'

'The night before Mark went on the trip. We were packing. It was his first school trip. In fact, it was his first time away from me, for nights, I mean.'

'I know.'

'His bed-wetting problem. I'd been worrying about it, what if he wet his bed in the camp. I'd been thinking about it, because at that time Dad or I always lifted him up, dead asleep, with the potty under his willy, at about eleven, and he peed, and then he didn't wet the bed in the night. If we were too late, a dinner party or something, the bed would be wet when we came to lift him out.'

'I remember all this, Mum.'

'So it was a real problem, for the trip. The teachers going on the trip were Mrs Mace, who was his form teacher, Miss Daniels, Mr Bose and Father Tree. So I had a word with Mrs Mace, I had a quiet word with her just to ask her if she could wake Mark and take him out of the tent to pee at about eleven. She said she would. She was totally understanding, and a very reliable person. I've never told you this before, because why would I? Anyway. The evening before going on the trip Mark was very quiet. You noticed it too. You told him he had trip-nerves, but he didn't smile. But we've talked about all this. Afterwards you suggested a premonition.'

'That's what people think at fifteen, of course it's nonsense.'

'While we were packing, I was trying to think of a way of telling him what I had done. I mean, that I'd had a word with Mrs Mace. Obviously, everything about bed-wetting is terribly embarrassing at the age of ten. But I knew he liked and trusted her. So I told him, and that she would pop into his tent at about eleven when everyone was fast asleep and lead him out and that he could have a pee in a hedge and all would be well. So no worries for him, I hoped. Now this is what he said. "Don't tell Father Rog." And he went quite white. Well, of course I wouldn't have, because Father Rog wasn't a mother, nor his closest grown up on the trip. But it was the way he said it. I said, "I haven't and I won't," something like that. And I imagined he had said "Don't tell Father Rog," in that urgent way, because – well, Father Tree was a bit of a hero, and he didn't want him to know about bed-wetting, out of totally understandable pride. That's what I supposed. So we went on packing, and then I took him to the coach outside the school, in the morning, and Mrs Mace whispered to me, "I haven't forgotten," and then I waved . . .' Betty could not go on. She broke down and cried.

Julia's heart sank. She had always disliked to see her mother cry, and had endured so much of it twenty years ago, then again, though less, a year ago. Tears had a way of making Betty's face settle in folds and creases you didn't know it had; and, for Julia, this had always been a daunting spectacle. At the same time she was intensely sorry for her mother, who had been through one of the worst things a mother can go through, and had done well. It was easier to admire her when she was not actually crying. Betty was not a person to have tissues or a hanky on her person, and Julia resignedly went off for kitchen paper from the roll. She introduced some sheets into Betty's hand, and crouched down beside her chair, putting an arm round her shoulders. She saw a mole she had not noticed before on her mother's neck, but after a quick peer was able to exonerate it. She waited. Whether there was any substance in Betty's fears of what might have happened to Mark at the hands of Father Tree, Julia could not know, though it seemed to her unlikely. She regretted Betty's feelings having been stirred up afresh, probably unreasonably, certainly uselessly. It was an issue for Julia, in her therapy, whether she had ever mourned her brother properly. When the disaster happened, she had been taken up with worrying about Betty and trying to make things better for her, and indeed, covertly, for Jack. Jack was more continent of emotion than was Betty. Continent or not, Dad had never been the same. There was also the question, for Julia, which had arisen for her at fifteen and was still unresolved, whether, for her parents, the wrong child had died and the wrong child had lived. What with all this, and GCSEs, mourning Mark had been difficult for Julia.

Julia felt Betty's shoulders stop shaking, as Betty pulled herself together. Betty used the kitchen paper on her eyes and nose. She said, 'Put on the kettle for a cup of tea, there's a darling,' and, as Julia moved to do so, Betty said, 'There's only one thing for it, I shall have to track down Roger Tree, and ask him some questions. That's the only way I'll ever find out.'

~

It had been the May half term week in 1990. A group of twenty-four ten and eleven year olds from St Malachy's were going on a school trip. There was excitement. They were going to learn the basics of camping. Eight tents of a reasonable size had been delivered to the school, six for the twenty-four children; two for the four members of staff. Mrs Mace and Miss Daniels would have a tent; Mr Bose and Father Rog another. There was joking among the more sophisticated children about the apportioning of tents among the adults possibly being other than expected, for Miss Daniels was thought to fancy Mr Bose. There would be four children to a tent; four was a good number. With billets of only three, there would be the danger of best friends being separated.

St Malachy's had never embarked on this enterprise before. It was Miss Daniels' initiative. She had been a Girl Guide. To her, camping was very important. Swimming was important to her as well. Only swimmers were being allowed on the trip, for the camp site was beside a big river. They would hear the river from their beds, said Miss Daniels. Birds would be studied. Anyone who had binoculars should bring them. A coach would be at their disposal throughout. Father Rog was licensed to drive it.

There were also boats, slow, chugging motorboats, which they might even have goes at steering. Currents could be learned about, and the fact that all rivers seek the sea. A member of staff and six children would be allocated each boat. Perfect behaviour was expected on the water so that no one would be endangered. Misbehaviour would involve one entire boat being penalised, and a teacher and crew would be landlocked while the other three boats chugged happily off. No one wanted to be the author of this calamity. Boats could be moored near Roman remains in one direction, and, in the other direction, harboured at a town where a castle could be visited, and snacks and perhaps presents to take home might be found. There would be sausages and marshmallows to cook on the camp fire. Much depended on the weather.

On the eve of departure, after school, there was a meeting for staff and children involved in the trip. Roger, looking at Mark Winterborne, asked for a volunteer to help him check out the coach's engine. Mark jumped up happily, and while the other three adults and the rest of the children looked at a map in the school hall, Roger and Mark were together in front of the school where the coach was parked. Roger opened the engine. His heart was pounding. He could feel Mark's light body leaning against his own as they peered in. Roger pointed out and named different parts of the engine and their functions.

Then Roger said, 'Now I'm going to be very naughty and have a cigarette. Shall we sit in the coach while I smoke it? Then we can go back and find the others.'

Mark was excited to be with Father Rog in this slightly clandestine way, and he watched while Father Rog lit his cigarette. They were sitting in the front seat of the coach, Roger on the inside, Mark on the outside. Then, smoking, Roger began to speak.

'I don't think there can be anything wrong in telling you how much I like you. I like all the children at St Malachy's, of course. But there's no harm in telling you I like you in a special way. I love you. I think God has given me this special feeling for you, and I hope he will use it for his own purposes.'

Mark said nothing. He liked being special to Father Rog. He had hoped he was. He was not so sure about love. That word from Father Rog gave him a shivery feeling he did not like. It was worse when now their eyes met, and Mark saw a moist yearning in Father Rog's eyes. He had liked Father Rog – loved him perhaps – because he was young and manly and good at things. Mark did not feel Father Rog's face looked manly at this moment, in spite of the cigarette. But Mark was too polite to jump up and run to join the others, which he would have liked to do, or even to suggest they both should do so. He watched Father Rog's cigarette and hoped it would soon be finished. Something in him was hurting, as if it was injured.

'You're not embarrassed, are you, Mark, if I talk to you like this?'

'No, Father Rog,' said Mark.

Now Father Rog took Mark's hand. He waved it about a bit, as if he was being hearty, rather than sissy-ish. 'So we're friends?' said Roger.

'Yes, of course,' said Mark. He pulled his hand away, when he could, and they went to join the others and the map.

~

The first evening at the camp, never again to be used for a school trip, was exciting. The tents were erected, and, seeing him busy and strong, helping everybody, having a laugh, Mark managed to get back some of his old, nice, unworried liking for Father Rog. Then there was the camp fire. There were sausages and chicken wings. Everyone sat round the fire. The rain had held off. There were songs. Mark was sitting with his best friend, Artie. He hoped that Father Rog could see that he had a best friend, and did not need a grown up one.

The children dispersed to their tents, shooed along by the staff, and after a brief hubbub, settled in their sleeping bags. 'Early night tonight, big day tomorrow,' said Mrs Mace. 'We'll be able to keep the fire in all night, unless it rains, and after cooked breakfast it's the boats.' She looked in to every tent to say goodnight.

All this was very exciting, and had the effect of making the children feel cooperative. They went to sleep.

The staff sat round the camp fire. They opened bottles of wine. Glasses had not been brought, so they drank their wine from mugs. Perhaps this was partly why they drank an amount which, when they saw the empties the next morning, surprised them. They were people who already knew and liked each other. Roger was the least well known because of not being one of the teachers; but, as a very available chaplain, he was popular with the staff. They conversed in a quiet, intimate, desultory way. They talked about their childhoods. They looked at the stars. Roger pointed out which was which.

'Golly,' said Mrs Mace suddenly. 'Mark hasn't had a pee.'

No one knew what she meant, so she explained. 'I don't think I can do it, I'm too tipsy,' she said with an unattractive giggle. 'What about you Rog? You just have to help him lift up, get him out of the tent, and let him have a pee. He'll do it more or less sleepwalking, his mum says.'

Roger stood up in the dark. Of course he knew which was Mark's tent. He even knew where Mark's sleeping bag was in that tent, luckily nearest the opening. Roger lifted the sleeping child, extricating him from his sleeping bag, not without difficulty, and carried him clear of the tents. His heart was pounding. He pulled down Mark's pyjama legs. He held them back, so that they would not get wet if Mark peed. He waited.

'Are you awake?' he said to Mark. No answer. But he saw Mark's penis straighten slightly as a stream of pee poured steadily out. Mark's body was limp with sleepiness.

'Wake up, Mark,' said Roger. 'We've got to get you back into the tent.'

Mark began to wake up, still supported by Roger's arm. 'I want a pee, too,' said Roger, unzipping his trousers. Mark was fully awake now, and could stand by himself. Roger's penis was too stiff for him to be able to pee.

'Will you touch my willy?' he said to Mark. 'It's too big like this, and I won't be able to pee.'

Horrified, but polite still, Mark touched Roger's penis. He tried to pretend this was not happening, as he did at the dentist. It did not take much to make Roger come, and, though Roger tried to direct the ejaculation away from Mark, he was not entirely successful. 'Now we must go back to your tent,' he said.

Mark crawled into his sleeping bag. It was still warm, warm as if nothing had happened. He lay down, his arms crossed on his chest, holding himself, each hand gripping the opposite shoulder. There was smelly slime on his pyjama front, he had stubbed his toe on a tent pin, he had trodden on a slug. Everything was horrible now. Perhaps it had been a dream. It had not been a dream. Mark began to sob.

Ayleen had been woken by the activity in the tent, and now heard Mark crying. She pulled herself out of her sleeping bag, and crawled over to Mark. 'Don't cry, Marky,' she said. 'It's all right.' How could Ayleen know that it was not? She stroked his hair, and said, 'You want your mum.'

This too was true. Mark cried more, thinking how true this was, and how he should never, ever have left his mum to come on this trip. Ayleen began to shiver and went back to her bed. In the end Mark cried himself to sleep.

~

Roger caroused no longer, but sought his tent, in which Mr Bose soon joined him. Now that the fleeting exhilaration was over, Roger was miserable, horrified and ashamed. There was no sleep for him. He knew that he had done irreparable harm. He wished he could die. At this time he was twenty-eight, in his first parish, and now, tonight, his priestly life was over. Mark would tell someone, and that would be that. Roger stood to lose everything. He wanted to concentrate on the damage he had done to Mark, but his mind kept sneaking back to himself, wondering how to handle the consequences. He hated Mark now. He hated himself for hating Mark, but then he only hated Mark more. Sometimes a gentle breeze blew through his alcohol-filled brain and said all this might blow over. In the morning the child would have forgotten. He was not properly awake anyway. At other moments Roger prayed for forgiveness. It was a long night. He struggled out of his sleeping bag, un-refreshed, in the grey of early morning, the first to be up and about. He looked at the river and thought about drowning himself. He had done to a little one what deserved a millstone.

The four members of staff became fascinated by rekindling the camp fire and trying to cook breakfast. Omelette had been the idea, and there were big frying pans. The pans were balanced on twigs above flames or above embers. Nothing was very satisfactory, but all was engrossing. The embers were not hot enough, and the flames threatened to blacken the eggs. Some of the wood was wet, and smoke got in the eyes of the cooks. At first they did not notice a knot of children at the water's edge. Then voices started calling for someone to come. All four adults answered the call, and in a second everyone in the camp was thronging that particular piece of shore.

In the middle of the river, beyond where the motor boats were moored, there was a rock. It had a flat top, and the water lapped it, flowing across it quite rapidly. On the rock stood Mark, looking frightened.

'A few of us got on the boats,' said Patrick, 'messing about, but only a tiny bit, miss. We talked about what if we could get on to the rock. We didn't mean it. We never would have. Then Mark jumped.'

'How deep is it?' asked someone. Everyone could see that Mark was in danger of losing his footing. 'I'm going in,' said Roger. He tried to kick off his boots. Roger saw Mark stare at him blankly, but before their eyes could meet Roger looked away, in case his own eyes said too clearly, 'I want you to die.'

Roger slid in to the river. He made a splash that increased the flow of water over the rock, and Mark lost his balance and fell. His light body went fast downstream. Swimming vigorously, Roger pursued him. Roger's duffel coat was heavy with water, his boots, which he had not had time to pull off, filled immediately, and he was impeded by reeds entangling his legs. He only touched Mark once, and didn't manage to grab him. The campers, in a bevy, were running along the bank, following the swimmers. Sometimes they could see them, sometimes they could only see Father Rog. Then they couldn't see Mark at all.

The bodies were caught and stopped by a reedy outcrop of land, and the teachers, knee-deep in mud, pulled the two of them on to the shore. Roger responded to first aid and the kiss of life, but Mark did not.

Chapter 5

Ofsted was over. Another weekend, and Romola was able at last to foresee having time for her novel. Time there was, but inclination had faded.

She had given Roger the job of opening a bank account for Carina, and Roger had also been put in charge of the selling of Hereward's stone collection. After all, Roger had nothing to do, except periodically report to the police. He settled to his jobs in an eager, penitential spirit, and the estimated figure for the stones had been encouragingly high. They were to be sold at auction as soon as possible.

'Next there are the rings,' said Romola to Roger. 'Now they really will raise money. There's diamonds in there, and everything. The stones and the rings together will bring in enough for the moment. I don't suppose the watches will do so well.'

'Do you think I could have one of the watches?' asked Roger.

'Yes, of course. But take a cheap one.'

'I won't know the difference.'

'Take any of them, then,' said Romola, turning away.

'I didn't even know he had these collections. And here's us, selling them off.'

'Hereward wouldn't mind,' said Romola, her face twisting with grief. 'Now you go and do something, Rog, I've got to get on.'

'I'll cook supper tonight,' said Roger. He always did, and it was really rather convenient.

~

Hereward's move into his private specialist unit had been terrible. Romola had decided it should be she, rather than Carina, who went on the ambulance journey with him, in case Hereward would not like Carina to see him so diminished. Carina had not demurred. Romola had been struck more than before by Hereward's corpse-like condition, and had seen in a closer perspective how many tubes and machines it took to keep him ticking over.

'Will he get better – better than this?' she whimpered, when Mr Bleaney came to say goodbye to her.

'We never say never. But your brother's brain sustained an enormous insult. On balance the chances were he would pass away then and there. But he survived. He must have a very strong will to live.'

Because of Carina, thought Romola. Poor Hereward. All his life he had had passions for unsuitable women. The three of them, Hereward, Romola and Roger, hadn't been much good, in their different ways, in the matter of love. Why had it been so? Mum had minded having no grandchildren.

Mr Bleaney went on, 'As I've said to you before, there is considerable brain damage, which could not be reversed. There would be quality of life issues.'

'He'll definitely never write again?'

Mr Bleaney was silent for a moment, digesting the understatement of this question. 'We can definitely say that,' he answered.

'So wouldn't he be better off dead?' asked Romola, the words sounding brutal to her ears.

Not to Mr Bleaney's, for he was familiar with relatives' anguish, and the forms it took. 'That's not the way to look at it,' he said. 'Try to be positive. You must see how he does in Mayton Road – that's where he's going, isn't he? They will have all his records from us. We've asked them to keep us in the picture. I'll always be interested. I'm just so sorry it happened as it did. The surgery went very well.'

Having exonerated himself afresh, Mr Bleaney shook Romola's hand and hurried off, leaving her to make the nightmarish journey with Hereward to Mayton Road, comforted, insofar as she could be, by the calm of the nice paramedics, who took for granted that she was Hereward's wife.

They were greeted by the hushed tones and soft carpets of the private sector. Whether Hereward was more comfortable was, of course, impossible to say. Romola's visits did not persuade her that he was getting different or better medical and nursing attention. But perhaps he did not need it. Where he was, he was welcome, rather than a bed-blocker; when the weather permitted, the morning sun streamed in to his room; probably the situation was as good as it could be.

~

Romola sat at her desk. She tried to think about Molly Gibson, now without Cynthia, and about Roger Hamley, temporarily overseas. She knew, from the notes on the ending culled from Mrs Gaskell's advance publicity to daughters and friends, that outcomes were to be happy, and as expected. That suited Romola. But she felt that Molly should have a test of love for Roger, like a proper Victorian heroine. Romola had arrived at the idea that Lord Hollingford, the gauche, widowed son of Lord and Lady Cumnor, should fall for Molly, and Molly should refuse him for Roger, to the horror and disbelief of Mrs Gibson. There were two other things Romola intended to put right. One was the tiresome tendency Molly had acquired in the later chapters of the book to be ailing, or, in Mrs Gaskell's words, 'not strong'. That phase would pass, and Molly would be robust and healthy, walking tirelessly and unafraid of draughts. Romola also wanted to reconcile Dr and Mrs Gibson, and had decided that at some point – perhaps at the very end – Mrs Gibson should become ill. She would become mortally ill with cancer, though it would not be called cancer in the language of the book; and Mrs Gibson's courage in the face of death would impress her husband, and make him loving, no longer cold and sarcastic. The book could end with her funeral, with everyone present. Or should it end with Molly and Roger's wedding? Which would be the better ending? Both must happen.

These ideas had excited Romola a few weeks ago. But that was before the catastrophe of Hereward. It was before the shock of Roger. Now, as she sat at her computer with what she had already written in front of her, the ideas she had enjoyed so recently lay in her mind without stirring. She realised that what she really wanted to do was to read Hereward's manuscript. It was not that she wanted to read rather than write a novel, nor even, exactly, that she wanted to read a novel of Hereward's that she had not yet read, though this had ever been something to look forward to. What she wanted was to feel close to Hereward. The best way to feel close to him, perhaps, was not to sit beside his inert body in Mayton Road Special Unit, but to read what he had been writing in the last six months of his life.

It was a love story – of course. It took place in Italy. The modern part of the story, unsurprisingly, told of the miraculous love of a tired old Englishman for a Carina lookalike. It was vividly and intensely described, as was expected of Hereward. There was more overt sex than usual – Romola hoped this was autobiographical. Stories from the Italian Resistance were woven in and out of the present-day situations. The Carina lookalike, Marta, had ancestors, many of whom had been partisans. One of the themes of the book seemed to be that modern Italy had not lived up to the heroism it had produced so prodigiously during the war. Or perhaps this was not to be understood just in terms of Italy, but as a parable for the modern world. Romola was struck by the extent and detail of Marta's web of forebears and collaterals, and of her present-day extended family. This was fiction, Romola was sure; had Carina had such a family Hereward would have held forth about it. So many Italian names. Dates, including the month. And such a terrible lot of Italian place names. She must find a map. There were family trees at the back of the manuscript, presumably intended as appendices. Seeing these, Romola sighed and smiled. Hereward had covered sheets of ring-binder paper with intricate genealogies of their Hanulaland families, hers as well as his own. They went back several hundred years. To Romola these were unnecessary, and distracted from the essentials of the game. She had sighed and waited. However, it was she who kept the genealogies, along with the equally unnecessary dynasties of the kings and queens of Hanulaland, and had hung on to them, through house-moves and clear-outs. Perhaps she could look at that thick wad, one day, to feel close to Hereward.

Romola was skipping. She could not bring herself to read about and try to imagine the complex relationships between different Resistance groups, nor the build-ups to the various stands they took against Mussolini and against the Germans, under-equipped and hungry in beautiful Italian countryside. It was too much like hard work. A sneaking feeling grew in Romola that if this book were by an unknown author it would not be published. It would be published, of course, because it was by Hereward. Literary London knew that Hereward lay in a coma. It would probably give this novel the Booker prize.

Romola felt a qualm that the Carina character was called Marta, and feared a play on words. Was Marta going to come to a sticky end, heroically, as quite a few of her fictional forebears, one also called Marta, seemed to have done? Romola decided she must read the book properly, not give in to the temptation to skim through it or to look at the ending. She owed it to Hereward. So she settled down to read.

~

Carina visited Hereward, sometimes with her dear Padre, sometimes on her own. The Specialist Unit was less intimidating to her than the hospital had been. It was smaller, and more like a house. She learned easily how to find her way to Hereward's room, and became a familiar sight to the nurses. She identified herself, if she was invited into conversation, as Hereward's fiancée. Everyone was over any wonder they might have had about the age gap. People were sorry for her, but guessed she would quickly move on.

Not as quickly as all that. Carina had a stouter heart than some observers assumed. She sat by Hereward's bedside although nothing interesting ever happened. She sat by Hereward's bedside and did her nails, the process benefited by the bright light from some of his machines. At first she thought the nurses would think badly of her if she did her nails, and for a number of visits she sat doing nothing. But Hereward had liked to watch her do her nails, and, if it was not wrong in relation to Hereward, what did it matter if the nurses thought she had a cold heart? Actually, they did not. They found it a touching sight.

When Roger came with her, she sat, and he stood, never removing his coat. Sometimes he would try to have a word with a doctor or a nurse. Carina never did.

'He dreams,' she said to Roger. 'I think Hereward is dreaming.'

'I'm afraid not,' said Roger. For him, in his disgrace, the total obliteration of Hereward's mind was timely. He did not want it mitigated.

'You don't know, Padre,' said Carina. 'Hereward had wonderful dreams. They were very long. He always told me them in the morning when we woke up. Sometimes we were running from Germans, hiding in the mountains. It was very exciting. His dreams were like stories. Sometimes he was with Romola. Padre, why has Romola never married? Is she a virgin?'

'I don't know. You must ask her.'

The outrageousness of this idea made Carina go pink. 'Another question,' she said. 'You are a priest, but you never do priest's work. When do you say Mass? I would come to Mass, perhaps, if you told me where.'

'I'm having a rest,' said Roger, feebly. 'I'm not saying Mass, at the moment.'

Carina accepted this, though she thought it peculiar. She turned back to Hereward, and touched his hand. 'When you are not here,' she went on to Roger, 'I sometimes remind him of some of the dreams he had. The ones I remember. If he is dreaming, a dream might wake him up.'

'I don't think so,' said Roger. 'But go ahead.'

For Carina, visiting Hereward was at least something to do. She had a lovely house to live in. She kept the heating turned up in all the rooms. She was comfortable. And now she had a bit of money. But she had nothing to do.

She slept late. But there was still the afternoon and the evening to get through. She found a site on Hereward's computer where she could play games of patience, which she enjoyed. On Tuesdays the cleaner came. Carina didn't like the cleaner to see her doing nothing, but she had nothing to do. She watched cookery programmes on TV, and programmes about people looking at houses. She went to the shops, and bought something to cook for her supper. Sometimes friends of Hereward's remembered her and telephoned with offers of a visit or dinner or a weekend with them at their country house, but she did not want to see them. It had been all right when she met them with Hereward, but they were old and clever. She would have liked to buy clothes, and had been on wonderful clothes shopping expeditions with Hereward on Rosslyn Hill, just round the corner; but Romola warned her not to spend too much money. Carina was still afraid of Romola. Once she had dared say to Romola, 'Hereward would want me to buy clothes.'

Romola looked at her, kindly Carina thought, and answered, 'I'm sure he would. We'll see, in a little while. We'll see how much the ring collection brings in.'

Carina would have liked to look at the rings. She could have tried them on. But Romola kept that cupboard locked. Carina was afraid it was because Romola thought she would steal a ring. Roger had already taken a watch. Romola had given Roger a key to Hereward's house, so both Romola and Roger had keys now. Carina listened when she heard a key in the door. Either it would be Roger, and she would be pleased, or it would be Romola, and she would quickly turn off the TV, and pretend to be reading. She kept a book handy for that purpose.

Indeed she had tried to read some of the books in the shelves. Her reading of English was not good. Between that, and the fact that she was not a reader by inclination or experience, she failed with *Kidnapped*, whose title had attracted her, and with *A Passage to India*, chosen because she had seen the film. She came back

59

from the shops with magazines, sometimes, and had found a shop that sold Italian ones. Sometimes she thought Hereward would be sad to see her as she was now, and thinking that made her cry.

She talked to her mother on the telephone. Arriving at the house unexpectedly, Romola had seen Carina on the telephone in full Italianate mode, and was afraid she was running up a huge bill. But she said nothing, because the poor girl needed someone to talk to, and had no friends in London, unless you counted Roger. Romola was touched that Carina went faithfully to sit beside Hereward, but felt something must be decided about her. If Hereward were to die, say within the next year, Carina would inherit a fortune. But if he continued to live, if you could call it that, and his house had to be sold to pay for his care, Carina would be homeless, her inheritance would dwindle, and would ultimately disappear altogether, leaving Romola to pay for Mayton Road out of her own pocket and Hereward's literary legacy. At some point Carina would have to make decisions. Not knowing what was going to happen to Hereward made things so difficult.

'Hereward said if he died I should go home to Genoa,' Carina told Roger. But that was if he died. As things were now, Carina did not think about the future. She went on from day to day. She was waiting. Perhaps she did not know it, but she was waiting for Hereward to be himself again.

~

Betty, with the help of Julia, had convinced herself that it was highly unlikely Mark had been molested by Roger Tree. Julia reminded her how, when a friend is on a trip to Africa, and one hears of a flood in that continent, one may fear for the friend's life, a fatality invariably disproved. The odds against Roger having interfered with Mark were too long. Betty was still in touch, vaguely, with some of the mothers from St Malachy's, and at this time she both received and initiated phone calls, stimulated by paragraphs in the local and other newspapers, and established that no one suspected her son had been abused. The sons were in their thirties now, as Mark would have been; and there was no reason why they would be shy to reminisce, if there were anything to reminisce about. The St Malachy's mothers had questioned them, and the response had universally been one of surprise. So Betty's heart was quieted. She had also established via these phone conversations that Roger had arrived at St Malachy's parish in 1988, so Mark must have known him, probably only slightly, for about two years before the tragedy. That agreed with Betty's impression. As she raked her memory, she thought with satisfaction that Mark had not had any opportunities to be alone with Roger. Mark did not serve Mass. Indeed the Winterborne family did not go to Mass, once their children's place at St Malachy's was secured. As a family, they had no contact with the parish.

All this revisiting of the past had arrived at no conclusions, and mercifully had not produced evidence leading to unbearable speculations. But, for Betty, it had stirred memories, and Mark's death occupied the foreground of her mind in a way it had not in recent years. It had always been there, but life had indeed gone on; and so had death, in the person of Jack.

She dreamed about Mark again. In the early months after the accident she had never dreamed of him, and had prayed to do so. Gradually dreams had come, but at first always of his face as it had been in the mortuary, small, pale and unearthly. Then dreams had come that took his continued existence, as well as his death, for granted. In one of the dreams, a happy one, he had been present as he was in life, and had said, 'Sorry I can't come shopping with you, Mum, because I'm dead'. And he had kissed her, warmly and casually, in his own way.

Now Betty was dreaming of him again. The dreams were different from either of the early crops of dreams. Now Mark was always in water. Betty and Jack had been to see the camp site twenty-two years before, and had spent a day walking and measuring. It was agony, but when it was over they were glad they had done it. They stood in turn at the end of one of the boats, and considered the jump on to the flat rock, and estimated the strength of the water as it plaited itself continuously over the grey stone. They conjectured whether Mark had tried to swim, or whether the current had immediately been too much for him. They walked downstream, retracing slowly the frantic dash of the children and staff, and examined the muddy promontory which had arrested the two bodies, and on to which the bodies had been pulled. They scrutinised the grassy bank on which Mrs Mace and Miss Daniels had essayed the kiss of life.

In Betty's dreams now, she was seeing something that in reality she had not seen. Mark's body was in the river, and was being carried rapidly downstream. There was always a noise of water. She could see his face, sometimes surfacing, sometimes submerged. Once, she called to him, 'Swim! Swim!' Once she lay flat in the mud and held out her hand to him. Once, she was on the reedy promontory and received his waterlogged body, heavy, dripping, and held it close. Once, her hand reached him, and she pulled him out, and he took a breath, as if alive, though his limbs seemed to have dissolved.

She suspected Julia thought she was brooding. So she did not talk about the fresh spate of Mark dreams to Julia, or to anyone. She did not say how much she was thinking about Mark. She missed Jack. Gradually, over the twenty years, she and Jack had ceased to talk so often about Mark. Probably that was natural, but she wished it had not happened. Jack was the only person who minded about Mark as much as she did. She would never find another.

She had persisted in the project of looking her loneliness in the eye, and discovered that loneliness was like bereavement, as well as like the other forms of pain with which she had already identified its kinship. That did not explain why the loneliness, and the fear of it, had been part of her life long before she had lost anyone she loved. Perhaps it was there, within her, because of what was going to happen, rather than because of what had happened. Perhaps the future as well as the past can mark the heart indelibly. Since Roger Tree's eruption in the newspaper had revived the dormant anguish of Mark's death, loneliness had found its level, in the context of a more general and intense grief. It was merely an ingredient. Betty found she feared it less than before. She cut down on the restless manoeuvres undertaken to circumvent it, manoeuvres which actually made it worse. Wasn't there a hero – it was a Greek myth, probably – whose task was to hug a monster through fearsome changes, each worse than the one before, not letting go, until, finally, it became tame? She tried to remember the story. When the creature had exhausted its repertoire of frightening forms, it told you the truth, if you wanted to know it. Betty felt the stronger for this memory.

She still hoped to have a talk or correspondence with Roger Tree, but, thankfully, the project was not urgent in the way it had threatened to be. He had been with Mark at the end; that was all it was, now. Betty wanted, if possible, to go over those last ten minutes again, in the perspective of twenty-two years, with someone who had been there. Mrs Mace would do just as well, but she had long been lost to sight. Betty had googled a phone number for the local bishop, and tried it; but she was informed that Bishop Jenkins was on an extended break. Next she was going to write a letter, perhaps addressed to the bishop's secretary. She would ask whether Father Roger Tree could be given her email address. She thought that was better, less pushy than asking for his email. Perhaps he was in prison by now, she suddenly thought. But you were probably allowed to write emails from prison. It might depend on the prison. Or the email. She had no idea.

~

Now that spring had come, Julia thought Betty should go on holiday.

'You can afford it,' she said. 'Go somewhere sunny. I know! You could take a package tour, an arty or university one, so that you'd have congenial people. Think about it.'

'There's nowhere I want to go,' said Betty.

'There must be somewhere.'

'There honestly isn't. I thought now it's spring I would do the garden. Dad and I neglected it for the last year or two.' Gardening had nothing to do with keeping loneliness at bay. That might be its effect, but it was not its intention. Gardening was a proper activity. The pastimes that were set to drum up an illusion of company – they were the treacherous ones, creating more emptiness than they filled.

'You could do both. Spring and summer are quite long, put together.'

'I don't want to go somewhere I went with Dad, and I don't want to go somewhere I haven't been with Dad.'

'If you don't mind going in September,' said Julia, after digesting this obliteration of travel. 'You can come with me. I don't know where I'm going, or who with, yet, but it'll be somewhere nice.'

They left it there, for the moment. Betty was not sure she wanted to go on holiday with Julia, though it was tempting. It would be too easy to slide into a ready-made identity as Julia's mother, known to Julia's friends as the widowed dependant, with whom Julia was marvellous. Betty did not feel ready for this slippery slope, at sixty, if she ever would. Especially lately, with all this suffering, she felt she was becoming more of a person, and still developing. She was calling on muscle that in Jack's day she took for granted she did not have. Perhaps, she thought, she was getting ready for the truth her tamed monster might eventually utter. Or perhaps she was getting ready for death. Being looked after by Julia, however comfortable, could not be part of these enterprises. So Betty tied herself to the mast, and voyaged on.

Chapter 6

Roger was not yet in prison. He reported to the police on a regular basis, and continued to await his hearing.

He had not written the letter to his parishioners, although he still intended to, and sentences for it passed through his mind. 'I want to assure you that I did not offend in the time I was with you at Our Lady of Calvary, but only . . .' That was true, but seemed unbearably feeble. 'If you are a priest who has offended in this way, and put it behind him, you become an ultra hard-working and conscientious priest, to atone, and that very fact makes the offence more shocking when it comes to light.' Why should his parishioners want a tour through the sociology of clerical abuse? And how can you ever be sure you have 'put it behind you'? 'All I can say is that I am desperately sorry to have let you all down.' Well, of course he was. They did not need to be told that.

'I did not offend in the time I was with you at Our Lady of Calvary, but only . . .' He could not truthfully end that sentence with the words, 'but only at my previous parish'. He had offended in both his previous parishes. His offence against Tony Tremlow had been brought to light. His earlier offence, in his first parish, against Mark Winterborne, had not.

This was what was starting to vex Roger's conscience. He began to realise that he had never properly thought about Mark. It seemed incredible, but so it was. Busy and enthusiastic, reassured by his popularity, pulled back immediately into the maelstrom of parish matters, respected for an attempt to save a child's life,

Roger had not lived with his crime against Mark, nor its terrible sequel. He had recovered, not repented. To say that Mark's death was water off a duck's back for Roger would be too strong, but it was soon water under the bridge. His attempts to airbrush into coincidence the link between the transgression and the accident were not entirely a failure. He had gone to confession in Westminster Cathedral, where, amongst the many confessionals, it was easy to find a stranger. He and the elderly Spanish visitor to London, whose own temptations against celibacy had not taken the form either of males or minors, had a long talk through the dark visor, the queue outside building up unregarded. Roger pointed out that, because of Mark's death, he had got away with it, and could continue to do so; and that this was a source of guilt, as well as of relief. The confessor was not sure that this constituted a reason for Roger to go to the police. Roger must consider the massive upset, and, indeed, possible trial of faith, that this would impose on the boy's family, who had already suffered so much. Roger thought it best not to disclose that the family, being agnostic, had no faith to be tried, and listened to the heavily accented words with gratitude and lightness of heart. The matter was left to his conscience. Meanwhile, nothing like this must ever happen again. Could Roger be sure of that?

'Oh yes, Father. It wouldn't. It couldn't. It won't. How could it?'

That was twenty-two years ago. Roger knew he would be treated differently today. He applauded that difference, but had always thanked his lucky stars he had escaped its application.

These days Roger had plenty of time to think. One of the things he marvelled at was that he was not more crushed than he was. His life was utterly ruined, but he went about Romola's and Hereward's houses, the streets, the shops, Mayton Road Special Unit, and a church, as if he were a normal person. He was in disgrace with his beloved profession, and on the wrong side of the law. He was a sinner and a pervert. He faced a jail sentence, probably of roughly four years. And yet he could smile. Why, he wondered? Perhaps it simply had not hit him. Did he not believe this was happening to him? Or was it that you get used to anything? Was it relief? His abuse of Tony had dogged him with anxiety, rather than with remorse; at any moment Tony might take it into his head to spill the beans. For twelve years Roger had lived on the slopes of an active volcano, and, as clerical abuse became an open scandal, the rumbles increased. He tilled the land, as if all was well; but at any moment the cataclysm could come. Now that the worst had happened, Roger no longer suffered that suspense. That weight, at least, had been lifted from his shoulders, even if worse had been placed upon them.

He had never had that anxiety where his first act of abuse was concerned. Indeed he used to feel a glow of satisfaction when he mulled over the fact that no one knew. There were no witnesses, no suspicion. You did not have to count the priest in confession, for he was bound by the seal of the confessional. The feeling of safety had been like being warmly tucked up in bed, himself and his secret as snug as a bug in a rug. Yet he had believed he was penitent, had thanked God for saving his skin, and had resolved to live a better life.

He dreaded prison, at the times when he was able to make it real to himself that he would actually be there, and soon. He suspected he would be the sort of prisoner who has to ask for solitary confinement because boiling soup is poured down his front by the fellow-prisoner serving the meal. Roger had always been valued, loved even, in the groups he had been part of. This would be the first exception.

He received an email from Bishop Jenkins.

'Hi, Rog,

I am billeted in a convent in Cumbria, a very small institution in a very beautiful place. Things are looking up for me. Apparently – grapevine – Gerard Farrell has a criminal record! I didn't know whether to believe this or not. It seems too good to be true, as it may lower his credibility in the eyes of the police. I'm not sure that it's right that it should, and if I was guilty, it certainly wouldn't be right! Anyway, there it is. But then I got a letter, forwarded to me here, from his mother. I remember her, do you? She asks how much money I would be prepared to pay for Gerry to withdraw his accusation! I handed the letter to the police. I hope the police are having second thoughts about me. What a ghastly time. But I've got my hopes up now.

Meanwhile I wonder how you are getting on. It's worse for you. At least for me my conscience is clear. I do get angry and frustrated. I am reading quite a lot – the convent library – chaps like Ronnie Knox and Frank Sheed, dated, but still sound, and interesting. Then they've got Rahner, Teilhard, that lot. It's refreshing. Let me have a line about you. I guess you are still with your sister. Awfully sad to read in the paper about your brother.

The nuns like having me here, because they get Mass every day. I don't think many of them realise why I have been put in cold storage! The sister-in-charge knows all about it, and, I think, believes me. I am not allowed to say a public Mass, or preach, but I regard eight elderly nuns – nine, if the one of 102 feels well enough to come to the chapel – as falling within the definition of private.

God bless, pray for me, oremus pro invicem,

Love
Pip

Roger's first feeling was of intense disappointment. Being in the same boat as Pip had been a comfort. Pip's upturn of fortune, jaunty tone and exclamation marks, afforded Roger a fresh wave of desolation.

Roger missed saying Mass. He was not debarred from attending it, however, and he sneaked into the back of Romola's local church, the location and existence of which Romola herself knew nothing, on Sundays, and, once he had established the times of services, on some weekdays as well. He stood in the shadows, afraid of being recognised. Someone had kindly welcomed him one Sunday, assuming he had newly moved to the parish; he had fled.

~

Julia felt as if there were two of her. There was the Julia who worked hard and cared very much about her career, who was rumoured to be in line for the next consultancy that came up in the Dermatology department at her hospital, who had a special research interest in subungual melanoma. That was the Julia who had taken this small, convenient flat. Then there was the other Julia, who heard the biological clock ticking, and wanted a baby more than anything else in the world. That Julia was not accommodated in the new flat. The new flat was no place for a baby. The right man would be able to reconcile the two Julias. But where was the right man?

However, nothing was lost. The flat was an asset, and could be sold easily, especially now it was enhanced by Tony's beautiful work. And what could she have done, but buy a flat to suit the career Julia? She could not afford a house, with a garden, in London, for the Julia with a baby. She did not want to move out of London, for her friends were there, her mother, her job. She had always lived in London.

'Have you always lived in London?' she asked Tony.

He had, and hoped he always would. Baz, his partner, was from New Zealand, but was well settled in London, and wanted it to be his permanent home. This topic led to a conversation about academic achievement, for Baz was doing a Ph.D. Tony had done well at school, until the Father Rog event. Then he had begun to fail. This didn't matter, for he was very happy with carpentry. But it was something else he held against Father Rog.

'That cuts both ways, though,' he said. 'I got really good at English because of Father Rog and the book group. So perhaps . . .'

One day Tony revealed to Julia how and why he felt guilty about Father Pip and Gerry Farrell. Another day, she disclosed that she, like him, was in therapy. It crossed her mind, as a crazy idea, that she might ask him for sperm. She did not do so. Her growing unreserve towards him did not include her desire for a baby; the life and death of Mark; or the fact that she knew anything other than what he had told her of Roger Tree. It seemed appropriate that she should know more of him than he of her. She was older, and, she hoped, perceived as wiser. The relationship was a pleasure to both. Neither seriously doubted that once his work in the flat was done, contact would end.

Julia prepared herself for a dinner-party. The trouble with being single, she thought, as she made up her face in front of the mirror, was that you had to have so much social life. She drove to her dinner-party, became fairly engaged in some of the conversation, did not meet a possible man, and drove home, sober.

Stan never went to bed before 3.00. That was one of the things that made him troublesome, if you lived with him. So she telephoned his number.

'Yes? Stanislaus here.'

'Hello.'

His voice changed. 'Julia! How lovely. What a treat. To what do I owe?'

She was pleased to hear him, too. 'Stan, it's about a baby.'

'Do you mean you are pregnant?'

'No, the opposite. I want to be pregnant. I want a baby. I am thirty-eight. I haven't got a man. Would you consider providing some sperm? Of course I don't mean sex.'

Stan was thinking this through. He was not a person to ask unnecessary questions. 'Aha,' he said, which meant he had become master of the material.

Julia waited for this moment to come. 'Any hope?' she said. 'I'm asking you first.' As a matter of fact, she did not have anyone else in mind, since the mad thought of Tony, but found herself impelled to pretend she had.

'Let me think about it,' he said. 'I'll have to see if Vicky is all right with the idea. We'll probably both have to think about it. Possibly you also have more thinking to do.'

'No. I've thought.'

'OK, leave it with me. I'll get back to you. I'm assuming this would be no strings fatherhood?'

'Absolutely no strings.'

'And how to do it. I suppose you would know. You would just have to collect from me, probably more than once, some warm, fresh ejaculate.'

It took Julia a couple of seconds to absorb the description; then she said, 'Exactly.'

'Now, how are you?' They talked about how they were for ten minutes, although it was so late. Julia went to bed excited about her project. She was also warmed and comforted by having heard Stanislaus's slow, accented voice, his deliberate, versatile English. An impossible man, a power-house of self-absorption; but how she had loved him, at first.

Chapter 7

Now Romola was dividing her time between school work, Mayton Road Special Unit and Hereward's novel. *Wives and Daughters* was languishing.

Roger had secured a huge sum for the stones, and was now in charge of the rings. Strange that Roger should be quite a good businessman; but Romola supposed a parish priest has to learn the skills of the real world, as he haggles a good price for church furniture or vestments.

Financially, Romola was not too worried for the moment. The fees of Mayton Road could be met, and Carina kept in comfort. Romola wished Carina had a friend. There had been a shopping expedition to Rosslyn Hill, Romola knew, but she doubted if it had been much fun for Carina, alone. And when would Carina wear the clothes, in the display of which Romola had tried to take an interest? They would increase the luggage Carina would take home to Genoa, or augment the rails in the already well-endowed Hampstead charity shops.

For Romola was beginning to accept that Hereward would not recover. In the past fortnight he had suffered – or not suffered, but been passive to – several cardiac arrests, any of which might have been the end of him. They had not been, to Romola's intense relief. But why be so relieved? How did it benefit Hereward to go on in this way? There he lay, Hereward of all people, as if a statue of himself. Machines made him breathe, made his heart beat, introduced nourishment. Were the cardiac arrests Hereward's efforts to die, guerrilla or *partigiano* exploits, outgunned by science?

Or was he trying to stay alive? Either of these possibilities lent more agency to Hereward than he had, and Romola was beginning to realise this. Hereward was not trying to stay alive or trying to die. He was doing nothing.

Romola regaled herself with stories from the internet, and, occasionally, from friends, about people who had come round from comas, against all the odds, and after years. Their eyelids had twitched; a lip had stirred; they had raised a finger to confirm they had heard a voice. Oh, Hereward, if that could only happen. Please do it. Don't be afraid of the brain damage. You will still be you.

For Romola's three undergraduate years, she and Hereward had been together at Cambridge. They were in and out of each other's rooms and colleges, and shared a large circle of friends. Like anything out of the common run at a university, the Trees as siblings were interesting. They created a social focus. They were also hard workers, Romola in particular, who got a first – a fact she downplayed, because Hereward, the more starry of the two, was, when the time came, less successful. Hereward had pioneered Cambridge without Romola; but Romola, when she arrived, found a ready-made social circle awaiting her. Because Hereward's course was four years, and hers three, she never had to do without him at university. University was not, for Romola, an initiation rite into independent life. When Hereward and she came down, they lived together in a flat in Islington, Hereward writing, Romola teaching. Romola was the breadwinner.

These biographical facts may go some way to offer an answer to Carina's question, 'Why isn't Romola married?' Romola did not have to seek exogamy in order to find partnership. Her friends certainly attributed her lack of a husband to the primacy of her relationship with Hereward. But, as with all arrangements in a life, it was more complex than that, and a single explanation was not enough.

Carina's other question, 'Is Romola a virgin?' had a simpler answer, for, of course, she was not. Being solid, bespectacled and unadorned, with a face that showed she took life seriously, a confident voice, and a hint of the formidable in her demeanour, she was not to many men's taste as a lover. But two at Cambridge and two subsequently had attempted to take her up. She had sex for the first time because she thought she should know what sex was. She knew that her motive would make her discovery meaningless, for she did not love the young man, and sex without love told you nothing, or not at the level at which she was curious. Despite his unimportance to her, the experience was potent enough to hurt, and the boyfriend's greedy inexperience made it a point of pride not to want him again. She laughed with Hereward over this adventure, and their laughter took a sting out of it. Other skirmishes followed, but she could not make them matter to her earnest heart, nourished as it was on love poetry, Shakespeare, and Victorian novels. She did not fall in love. There was a colleague, in the Islington period, who was really very nice, although Romola could well see why Hereward poked fun at him. Romola had an affair, and she felt more at home with sex than she had before or since; but he left her for another fellow-teacher who was readier to settle down. The idea of wanting to live with him, rather than with Hereward, had Romola chuckling at its absurdity.

Hereward meanwhile did his best to fill his rooms in Cambridge, in Islington, and in his later more permanent dwelling with forerunners of Carina, and, of course, for the first couple of decades the age-gap was not so pronounced. After a year or two of the Islington flat, he had a successful novel published, and money came in. The moment arrived when both he and Romola thought it wise to buy properties, and could afford to. Hence their houses, hers small, his larger, in walking distance of each other. It was thus that they had lived ever since. It did not matter to Romola that Hereward could be abroad, for a year at a time. Their mutual dependence was not of the day-to-day kind.

For this was the other reason why Romola had never married. She was always busy. She had started her working life as an academic. Soon her active social conscience had moved her to seek a job in a secondary school. It was large, mixed, challenging and inner-city. There she had learned how to teach big groups of unwilling children. She moved on, and up the ladder. She was now head of English in another, similar school, and, at fifty-five, had decided this was the right position for her. She had no wish to be a deputy head or a head, though she was often talent-spotted for such posts. She liked her work as it was. It was lucky that her personality, or possibly her appearance, if these can be differentiated, carried a certain authority. This was innate, not learnt, and perhaps it is not something that can be learnt. Her lessons were engaging, but it was not only that. There was a tradition that you did not mess with Miss Tree. She told students on teaching practice, 'You have to be the most interesting thing in the room'. Often they could not achieve this, and struggled, or left, accordingly. They knew, though Romola didn't, that this was not Romola's only secret weapon. 'Miss Tree only has to stand waiting in front of a class and they shut up,' was said of her. It was true.

She enjoyed institutional politics, and was easily drawn on to committees and steering parties. All this kept her busy. She was on telephone terms with members of the Department for Education. She was interested in policies, in literacy, in young people reading, and she wanted to make a difference. She could be indignant, and was articulate. She relished controversy. As school teachers go, she was important. Then in the school holidays, and, if she had time at weekends, she wrote her novels. Her internal world was lively, teeming, and, for the most part, cheerful.

For five years, until and including her death, her mother had lived with her. This had called for fresh supplies of efficiency and organisation from hard-working Romola, though Hereward had helped. It was satisfying for Romola to be able to do this. She loved her mother and grieved for her. She still thought of her often, and, in relation to her, bewildered herself, sometimes, with the question: what is a life?

Fifteen years ago, she had woken up to the fact that she would not have children. As a young person, even as a child, she had always assumed that she would. But at forty, she took stock, and saw that she would not. That was not something her life held. It held other things, but not that. Once she got over the momentous fact that a huge section of life was to be absent from hers, she did not mind very much. It was clear to her that it was only the idea that she minded. She had not known babies, nor ever been attracted to one. She was not an aunt. Hereward had had a vasectomy, twenty years ago, to relieve the mind of a pregnancy-phobic girlfriend. It seemed strange to Romola that none of the three Tree siblings were parents. The three of them seemed to her to have come to not being parents by such different, such idiosyncratic routes; but there they had each arrived.

When Romola and Hereward played Hanulaland in the attic of their parents' house, Romola had been happy. It was not ecstasy, which she had never known, but the happiness that is forgetful of self, time, and pins and needles. Hanulaland stories came magically to mind, developed, were shared, and, in the sharing, were enriched. The air constantly trembled with possibilities. Her inventiveness and her emotions were worked to the top of their bent. Hereward's mind was congenial to hers, whilst being palpably other; and he didn't want more of a say in story or characters than she had. They each appreciated, often admired, the other's say, and both built it in to the joint narrative. They learned to notice and tolerate the emphases and predilections of another mind. Romola found Hereward a bit too keen on noble deaths and self-sacrificial speeches. On his side, the magic potion one of her characters was liable to produce at the last minute to save a life was unwelcome. Sometimes one or other was privately ruffled, but they very seldom demurred, and, if they did, they quickly gave in, Hereward as much as Romola.. The mutuality of the game was of its essence. Romola's happiness at those times felt quite ordinary, like the happiness that comes, unfelt, from having good health and enough to eat. But time had not proved it ordinary. A lifetime of leaner years was to follow. Writing her novels, and being with Hereward, had sometimes recreated some of that happiness; but the subsequent versions of it were comparatively dilute and unreliable.

'How are the rings going, Rog?' she asked, over supper. 'The stones won't last for ever.'

'Don't worry about money,' said Roger. 'The rings will be astronomical. The watches, as we expected, will only amount to a few thousand. But I've had someone round to value the pictures. Pretty astronomical, again. Of all our worries, money is the least.'

'You know Mayton Road is over two thousand a week.'

'Yes. But we are all right for three years, without selling the house, and including Carina's allowance.'

'Allowance, and bills. Don't forget her bills. They'll be high. Heating. Phone.'

'I've reckoned enough for them, I think.'

'How is she?'

'Sad and lost, basically.'

'She must be lonely, with no friends in London.'

'She didn't believe you liked her new clothes.'

'Oh dear, and I tried so hard. Rog, I never ask you about you. You seem to be taking it so well. I don't mean about Hereward, I mean about you. How are you, really?'

'I honestly don't know.'

~

Carina was indeed lost, sad and lonely. She was also bored, and worried because she was putting on weight. She was not sure how long she could go on as she was. She had begun to believe that Hereward was not going to change. So what was the point of her staying in London?

'What do you think I should do?' she asked Roger, as she often did. 'I miss my family. I have never shown you a photo of my family.'

'No. I would like to see that.'

Carina ran to the bedroom and came back with the photograph. She was clearly proud to show it to Roger. He was intrigued. 'Tell me who everyone is.'

Carina's well-manicured finger picked out figures. 'That is my father,' she said. But Roger's eye was caught by a boy, probably about twelve. He was sunburnt, and screwing his eyes up against the sun. He was wearing shorts. Roger asked the identity of all the family members, slowly, taking his time, so that his eye could dwell caressingly on the face and form of Alessandro, as the beautiful boy turned out to be called.

Carina took charge of the photograph again. 'So what should I do?' she asked.

'You told me that Hereward thought you should go home.'

'But that was if he died.'

'Perhaps you have to start regarding him as dead.' Roger was used to these conversations with Carina, but had not said anything quite as direct as this before.

'But that is too cruel.'

'All the same. It would not be your cruelty. We could let you know if he comes round.' Now it occurred to Roger that at this imagined, and probably imaginary moment, he would be in prison. But Romola would let Carina know if Hereward came round. Some time, thought Roger, he would have to give Carina some idea of his real situation, or what would she think when he suddenly disappeared? He dreaded telling her any version of the truth. Her theory, he knew, was that he was a valiant missionary priest, on a much-needed holiday, perhaps because of a tropical illness. He had not had the heart to contradict it. Perhaps it would be best if she assumed he had been recalled without notice to the mission field. But then, what if she saw his hearing and conviction in a newspaper?

'Shall we visit, later, Padre?' asked Carina.

'Yes, if you like. Quite soon, perhaps, because after school Romola will go. We don't want to all be there at the same time.' But why not? The idea of spacing visitors so that the patient can get the most out of each did not apply to Hereward. But Romola and Roger found themselves making arrangements as if it did.

Roger had got into the way of using Hereward's computer. Romola's was full of records, marks, and profiles, as well as her novel; and he was afraid of deleting something vital. Also, Carina liked it when he was in the house. His letter to Maria and the parish was perpetually on draft. He went into Hereward's study to have a look at it now, while Carina telephoned her mother.

~

Vicky had a very nice house, thought Julia, and Stan had gone up in the world when he exchanged her flat, the old one, for Vicky's house. Julia rang the doorbell. On the negative side, for Stan, perhaps, though perhaps not, were evidences of children, visible through the glass of the front door – a small bike; a school blazer hung over the bannisters.

Vicky came to the door. Vicky and Julia knew each other slightly, though that was not the link through which Stan had teamed up with Vicky, after he and Julia separated.

'What a nice house,' said Julia. She had not been to Vicky's before.

'Yes. We were lucky.' Julia knew that 'we' did not refer to Vicky and Stan, but to Vicky and her long-estranged husband, the father of the owners of the bike and the blazer.

Vicky led Julia into the sitting room and asked if she would like a drink. When this was dealt with they sat down.

'Stan is in,' said Vicky, 'and he'll come when we call him. He thought you and I should have a chat first.'

Julia was nervous, but collected. She was in what was to her a very odd position. But she had made her decision and was going to brave it out. 'It's a very unusual request, I know,' she said, 'to ask for sperm from a former partner when he is in another relationship.'

'Nothing's odd, these days,' said Vicky. 'I feel for you. I've got my children, and I certainly don't want another by Stan. He tells me you wanted a baby with him but he was against. So I feel for you.'

'More than against, I'd say,' said Julia. 'Adamant.' Vicky's manner, and the glass of wine on an empty stomach, were going some way to normalise the situation.

'My only problem,' said Vicky, who was also feeling the benefit of her wine, and refilled the glasses, 'is that Stan might get mysteriously fascinated by his new progeny, and always be round at your place, drooling over it, and then wishing he had stayed with you and you could bring it up together.'

'I hadn't thought of that,' said Julia. 'He specifically checked on the phone that it would be no strings. But I see what you mean. I mean, I can imagine that. Oh, dear.'

At this point a charming girl in school uniform came into the room with an exercise book. 'Sorry, Mum,' she said, smiling in response to the visitor's smile. 'Is this sum right? If it is, I'm cool; I will have got the idea.'

Glasses on and quick look from Vicky. 'It is right, darling,' she said. 'I think you've got the idea.' Exit Tamsin.

'Do they like having Stan in the house?' asked Julia. 'And does he get on with them?'

'It all seems to work rather well. We have his kids every other weekend, and all four are friends now. As to having Stan in the house, they like him, with ups and downs. Easier for Tamsin than Robbie. But I am happier, much happier, and that makes life easier for everybody.'

Julia's and Vicky's eyes met when Vicky said this. It was the first intimation from Vicky of love for Stan. Julia felt a stab of jealousy, or exclusion, or loss. But it was a subterranean tremor, compared to the emotions on the surface.

'We'd have to get a guarantee from Stan,' said Julia, 'that he wouldn't come and drool. And you'd need a guarantee from me that I wouldn't secretly want him to. I can give that. If I do get pregnant, I may very probably be forced to move into my mother's. Stan hates her, because he was so beastly to both of them when Dad was ill.'

'Stan doesn't like parents,' said Vicky. This was the first hint between her and Julia that Stan was difficult. They smiled at each other, in a way that was not far off a giggle.

'Stan will have to think of himself as a blood donor,' said Julia. 'You give a pint of an essential fluid, and don't have to know whom you've helped.'

'I'm not sure he could manage a pint,' said Vicky, and then they really did laugh.

'I'm prepared to risk it,' said Vicky. 'But I trust you. It'll be up to you not to let him get enthralled by whoever, if it comes off.'

'I promise.'

'I phoned Mo to check with her whether he was keen on babies or not. She said he took no interest in either of his own until they could talk. That seems a good sign.'

'It does indeed. Good thinking, to phone Mo.'

'What would be the procedure, exactly?'

Julia had worked it out. 'This is my idea of it,' she said. 'I keep an eye on my ovulation. When it peaks, I phone you and Stan. If you are free, you come over to my place, both of you. You and I have a glass of wine while Stan . . .' Julia's words petered out.

'Wanks into a saucer?'

'A bowl. A slightly warmed bowl. He brings it into the room where we are sitting. I seize it and dash for my bedroom, where a turkey-baster is awaiting, warm from the vicinity of the radiator. I put it in, and lie on the bed to let it settle, while you two let yourselves out of the house and go home, job done. Do you think that would work?'

'I don't see why not. Worth a try, anyway,' said Vicky, intrigued by the strategy. 'It sounds a bit lonely for you. Maybe we could hang around, and if you feel it's settled, all go out for a meal. I'm just worried about a baby-sitter at short notice. I still have baby-sitters. The children are twelve and nine. But Wendy next door is almost always in. I'll tell her why it's urgent.'

Julia was wondering if there was irony in the degree to which Vicky was normalising the project. She looked at Vicky's face, and did not see irony. She saw practicality. She saw response to administrative challenge.

'I'll call Stan,' said Vicky, and did so on her mobile. Stan could be heard coming downstairs. He opened the door and crossed the room to Vicky. He kissed her head and ruffled her hair. She reached for his hand. He looked at Julia, and could not resist flashing her a complicit smile, outside Vicky's field of vision, to which smile Julia's face remained wooden. 'You are here on an eccentric mission,' he said.

'Talks about talks for an eccentric mission,' said Julia, more embarrassed now Stan was in the room, but able to hide it. Seeing Stan, handsome, ingratiating, and overweight, reminded her more now of how much he had annoyed her than of how much she had loved him. But simultaneously she was sizing him up as a gene-provider, and liked the fact that he was tall, and that he had lovely big eyes and thick hair. Her lack of all these features might be counterweighted.

'Satisfied with what you see?' he asked her. This situation was sure to make him arch and jokey, and Julia had foreseen that.

Vicky was not pleased with this tone. 'I think we've decided we are OK with it. The only thing is, neither of us wants you taking an interest in the baby, if there is one.'

'It is the first time someone has told me not to take an interest in a baby,' he said, not realising it was time to drop the manner. 'Before, in my life, I have always been chastised for failing to take an interest in my offspring.'

'Well, this is different,' said Vicky, and the crispness of her tone made him look at her, then sit down, and look her in the face.

'I accept that what is required of me is required of me, and nothing more,' he said, to both women, but mostly to Vicky. 'I have no personal or emotional investment in this enterprise. I am doing it to help out an old friend, because I feel it churlish to say no, having been asked. And, of course, any action is conditional on Vicky's not objecting.'

'No strings,' Julia reminded him. She was thinking it was typical of him to use the possessive, in the spoken language. His English, so good, would never be colloquial.

'No strings.'

'We'll be holding you to that,' said Vicky. To avoid a coupling-up against the third corner of the triangle by Vicky and Stan, or, delinquently, by Stan and Julia, the couple that had formed itself was Julia and Vicky. That was safest, thought Julia, and Stan was too complacent and flattered to mind.

'That will not be hard. I am far from being a natural patriarch.' After this step back in the direction of archness, he added, coyly, but looking at Vicky for approval, checking from her face how far he could go, 'Perhaps I will write a column about it. I am desperate for subjects. This would be a very stimulating topic.'

'So long as you don't mention my name,' said Julia, arch in her turn. 'Think of my job. We wouldn't want gossip in the department.'

~

Of course there were undercurrents, thought Julia, as she set forth for home, not, actually, having been invited to stay for supper. But not all undercurrents have to surface. Some just disperse, overcome by the stronger flow of the water above, and are as if they had never been. Her project, she thought, had that kind of dominant flow.

Chapter 8

'Hereward is no worse,' said Carina to Roger, when they got back from the nursing home. 'He is no better, I suppose. But isn't it a good sign that he is no worse?'

'A good sign', noticed Roger. Carina's English was improving. Romola had arranged a spoken English class for her twice a week, or, more precisely, had organised Roger to arrange it. It gave Carina something else to do, and people to meet.

'I'm afraid not. They are keeping him going at the same level. It's all those tubes and machines.'

'He would not like it.'

'He certainly wouldn't.'

Carina began to cry.

'I'm sorry it's so sad for you,' said Roger, feeling this was weak. His own sorrow for Hereward's plight was contaminated not only by relief for what Hereward could not know, but also by a younger brother's secret glee at how the mighty had fallen. But when he visited Hereward, and stood by his bed, Hereward's utter helplessness pinched his heart. It was a terrible thing to happen to a person. Except for the tubes, Hereward's face looked like Hereward's face, and even rather healthy. That was the nutrients, probably, and the withdrawal of drink and cigarettes. His hands were particularly poignant. They were still folded, with every appearance of docility, upon his chest. 'Perhaps they should let him die,' he added, more to himself than to Carina.

'Let him die? Without all those machines, would he die?'

Carina spoke sharply, evidently shocked by a new thought, or by the formulation of a thought she had not quite had.

'Oh yes, of course.'

Carina was thinking. 'Then that must mean that God means him to be dead.'

Roger groped for his moral theology. 'God has enabled us to keep people alive by our scientific and medical advances. He intends these advances. So we can't say God wants these people to be dead.'

Carina was relieved. 'I would not like God to want him in heaven and us to stop him going there,' she said. Roger could not think of an answer, and after a minute Carina went on, 'Perhaps he needs a priest to take away his sins. You could do it, Padre.'

'He isn't a believer,' said Roger, aware that he was fencing.

'All the same.'

Roger took a deep breath. He was an unfrocked priest, not entitled to administer the sacraments, and Hereward was an atheist. 'Look, next time we go, if you want me to, I will say the words of absolution over him. Would you like that?'

Carina smiled her beautiful smile. 'Yes,' she said. 'Then, if he gets better, perhaps he will believe in God.'

'Anything is possible,' Roger conceded.

While Carina made coffee, he went to the computer in Hereward's study. He looked at his inbox. There was a message from the bishop's secretary. It gave him the email address of a Betty Winterborne, and told him that this lady would like him to get in touch with her.

His first, mad thought was that she had found out about his abuse of Mark. He needed to remind himself that this was impossible. Why would she want him to contact her? He could ignore the email, and was tempted to. His impulse was to hide, cover his head, and moan. He had enough trouble already. His fingers hovered, wanting to delete. Then a braver part of him made its voice heard, and reminded him that this was a woman whom he had terribly wronged, and to whom he owed whatever it was that she thought he could give her. At this moment, he did not rush in, as he usually did, to blur the link between his abuse of Mark and Mark's death, and he sat, still, serious and staring, until he heard Carina call, 'Coffee! Where are you, Padre?'

~

The next day, knowing Carina was at her class, Roger crept into Hereward's house and sat down at the computer. He entered Betty Winterborne's address, and wrote 'Renewing Contact' against the Subject.

'Dear' – should it be Betty, or Mrs Winterborne? He must have called her Betty, he supposed. Betty and Jack, memory suddenly supplied. 'Dear Mrs Winterborne, I hear you would like to write to me.' He deleted 'write to me', and substituted 'be in touch with me. Please feel free to contact me on the above email address.' Chilly to the point of cold, but he couldn't help it. 'I hope you and Jack and the family' – had there been a family? Risk it – 'are well'. 'Well'? Did that not suggest forgetfulness of the tragedy? But what other word was there? And Roger did not want to waste having remembered Jack's name. 'Yours, Roger Tree'. All you could say for the email was that it did its job. He wondered whether you could receive emails in prison. If not, the Mrs Winterborne problem might not have time to develop very far, and that not through his own fault. He had a date for his hearing now, though it was still two months away. His hair bristled with fear when he thought about it.

He was waiting to make a cup of tea for Carina on her return when his phone went. It was Pip Jenkins.

'Rog?'

'Yes.'

'I wanted you to be the first to know. The first outside official channels, I mean. I'm out of the wood.'

Roger's heart sank. 'That's wonderful news,' he said.

'Gerry Farrell has withdrawn everything. There is something about him being incited to accuse me falsely, I suppose by his family. I am very happy. I shall await orders, staying up here in the convent. I will be reinstated, though of course some of the mud will stick and I shan't be a bishop again. But I don't mind. I only hope I don't have to pen-push in the Vatican. If I can be the parish priest of people who can trust me, that's all I ask.'

That was all Roger could ask, as well. 'That's wonderful news,' he said again, stuck for words, because of loneliness, disappointment and envy.

'Luckily for Gerry, the case didn't get far, and he may not be done for wasting police time, though he is going on probation. He has a variety of petty crimes to his credit, I gather. The police are going to ignore his mum's letter to me, and I think that's right.'

'All that time you spent coaching him in maths. That didn't promote his career much.'

'Oddly, it probably did. I hear he was very good with safes.'

They laughed, Roger hollowly. 'I've got my date,' he said, 'the date for my hearing.'

'What an awful thing, Rog. I'm sorry. Have you any idea whatever possessed you?'

'You can't help who you are attracted to. For me it was boys, for you women. There it is.'

'Yes, but why children? Perhaps it's too painful to ask, I probably shouldn't.'

Roger knew Pip would not be probing if not disinhibited by euphoria. Pip was asking a question to which Roger did not know the answer. 'Both times I'd had a drink,' was all he said, which was no answer. 'If they'd give me another chance, I'd gladly take the pledge.'

'Twenty years ago, that might have been possible,' said Pip. 'Even ten. But it wouldn't be right, would it? I'll give you a bell again soon. I've got lots to do.'

'Thank you for ringing,' said Roger. He was not in the least grateful. Why had Pip thought he, of all people, should be the first to hear?

He heard Carina's key in the door. She was delighted to find him in the house, and he made them tea, which he was training

Carina to like. 'I am going shopping on Saturday,' she said, 'with a girl from my class. She is taking me to Brent Cross. What is Brent Cross?'

~

Spring was turning to summer, now, and Betty's garden was wonderful. It was hard to have to think of it as her garden, when it had been so completely hers and Jack's. It seemed to have thrived on the comparative neglect of the past two years. Everything was in blossom or in bloom. Betty stumped down the path to the shed to get the tools out. This had been Jack's job. He had always lined the tools up along the side of the shed for them to pick from. That was always a good moment, betokening a gardening Sunday. From Betty's point of view, that particular sort of companionship was perfect. It avoided the weight of either intimacy or solitude, whilst being full of affection and a shared task.

So she missed Jack, as she gardened. She missed Jack, but she was not lonely. The neighbour, peering through the fence, glad to see signs of life again, thought Betty a lonely sight. She thought of calling a greeting, but then she noticed that although Betty was a lonely sight, she was also a busy one. Betty must learn to get on with it alone, the neighbour realised, so she did not call Betty's name. Had she done so, Betty would have been grateful for the intention, but would not have welcomed the interruption. She would have felt unpleasantly discovered in an activity which was private, and which, in that it explored her questionable capacity to be alone, was tinged with shame. This well-intentioned call did not happen, and Betty worked quietly on, unconscious of having been observed. She pruned where growth was out of hand, and weeded where precious plants were struggling for life. She smelt the familiar smells of the different flowers, and the turned earth, and rejoiced in them. Jack had planted most of the bushes, except the roses, which had been inherited; so she felt close to Jack. Mark's ashes were in the earth under these bushes. Would it have been better to have a grave, which she could visit?

Jack passionately wanted what was left of Mark to be in the garden. Betty hated both burial and cremation for Mark too much to take a view. How could one seem better than the other? Jack took the decision.

Soon, though perhaps not today, Betty would have to drag out the heavy lawn-mower and mow the small lawn, always Jack's task. Not today, perhaps, for, when she had finished clearing, she would have to bag up the debris, a boring job, and a prickly one, and there was always more debris than expected. But the council collected garden rubbish now, and that was very convenient. She and Jack had got out the car and taken it to a distant dump. She would hate to do that alone.

There had been less contact between Julia and herself in the past days than usual. Betty was pleased to find she hankered less to see or telephone Julia. Betty had needed to discipline herself, but now it seemed that the need for discipline had abated. In the long evenings of the past year, she had often thought up laborious excuses to ring Julia. Now, not unusually, she managed to make herself comfortable alone. Not always. Sometimes she had to walk briskly round the block to feel in contact with the world, and she had considered getting a dog. But with a frequency known only to herself, and notable only to herself, there had been evenings when she had managed to read, quite pleasantly, until a respectable bedtime. One of Betty's friends said, 'You are never alone with a book'; but Betty always had been. Less so now.

Unless there was a programme she had circled earlier in the day, she did not turn on the TV. That was difficult. But it brought its rewards. She was sad, but she was stronger. She was less afraid. She did not place her ineffective sandbags against the rising tide of loneliness, but let loneliness flow in, its waters rising higher and higher, while she waited to see if she would drown. She did not drown. Sometimes, unexpectedly, she was in her depth. At other times, she swam, and learning to swim increased both muscle and confidence. She was less afraid, and she would go further next time.

One afternoon, when time hung heavy, she got out her paint

box. It was in the cellar, in the alcove where things were kept that would probably never be wanted. She sat on the steps to the garden and did a watercolour of the honeysuckle, burgeoning, pulling on its dilapidated trellis. She had not painted for years. When she came indoors, the picture finished, three hours had passed. This happened again, one evening, with a hastily concocted still life of a jug, an orange and a newspaper, on the sitting room window ledge, the curtains undrawn, framing it. Looking at both these pictures gave her huge satisfaction. Other people liked them too. Perhaps she would go to an evening class. A life class. Or perhaps she wouldn't; classes reminded her of defence against loneliness, in a way that painting did not.

She took to frequenting Mark's room. It was the larger of the two second floor bedrooms, and it looked out over the garden. She decided to do a painting of what Mark had seen from his window. The room had been in occasional use as a spare bedroom in the last twenty years, but bore little trace of any occupancy but Mark's. The bookshelf held his books, because, why not? Where else to put them, and how else to fill those shelves? The chest of drawers had been empty of his clothes for many years, and the cupboard of his toys. Those had gone to be useful at jumble sales. The single bed was where it always had been. One day Betty lay down on the bed, and looked at the sections of ceiling and wall that would have been familiar to Mark from this angle. She was revisiting all she could of his life, greedy now for the kind of detail towards which at the time she had been casual and hasty. They had just been part of ordinary life, then. How could she have known she must treasure them? Mark's bedtime ritual came back to her, in more detail than it ever had before. Memories unscrolled, now that she was letting them. She sat where she had sat to read him stories. She allowed herself to remember the times she had been too busy or too bored to do so, and had left him to go to sleep disconsolate. She remembered the potty, and she or Jack traipsing upstairs at eleven, to hold him over it, and the irritation on the occasions when they were too late. The light would be abruptly turned on, Mark skinny and shivering in a chair, Betty's brisk, hard-done-by, almost word-less changing of the bed, and of his pyjamas. Remembering his beloved teddy, George, was on the very edge of what she could endure. The teddy itself she did not see, for a visiting child had fallen in love with it, and Betty had bravely given it away, years ago.

She was able to wonder about Mark as a person, rather than feel him as a loss. She remembered and got interested in what remained in her mind of his games and preoccupations; his school friends; what he liked best to eat; the fact that he had so loved those rather tiresome Narnia stories. She found his mouse Reepicheep in the bottom of the bookshelf. She had not seen it for years. She put it in her pocket, and kept it. What would Mark be like if he was alive today, at thirty-two? There was no point in wondering that; and so she went back to the boy she had known, the baby, the toddler, the little boy, then finally the child of ten, when memories had to stop. She looked closely and at length at photograph albums she had avoided before. She looked at drawings and paintings and large-lettered pieces of writing she kept in a cupboard, Mark's and Julia's, too many from both; but you never throw them away, any more than you ever look at them. With one thing and another, Betty became occupied, and even busy.

One day in this period she looked at her email and there was Roger's message. Reading it – which she did three times, although it yielded so little – she felt uncomfortable rather than intrigued or relieved. Yet her project with regard to Roger belonged to her current state of mind. She wanted to know Mark better. She wanted to see Mark as a person. Roger had been close to him in the last twenty-four hours. Roger might produce other memories of him. She and Roger could have a conversation about Mark.

But she was daunted by the thought that he was in a bad way, facing prison, possibly already there. She would be expected to sympathise, or perhaps hear his excuses. She did not want to talk about Roger, but only about Mark. But courtesy might require her to listen to a tiresome saga that he would want to get off his chest to yet another pair of ears.

Her first impulse was to ring Julia, but she resisted it. She sat at the computer, thinking. Then she wrote:

Dear Father Roger Tree,

I am very much thinking about my son Mark at the moment. After the fatal accident, you kindly came round to visit Jack and me. Perhaps I did not thank you for that at the time, or for saying a Mass for Mark. I know I was grateful. I am also aware that it was you who put your life at risk in an unsuccessful attempt to save him. Thank you. At that time, it was probably impossible to be grateful for anything. I would love to hear any memories you have of Mark, if you have any, either from your time as chaplain to St Malachy's before the camping trip, or during the trip. My husband died over a year ago. I have few people now with whom to reminisce about Mark, which is what I like to do. A few email recollections would do very well.

Yours
Betty Winterborne

She had said nothing about Roger's present predicament, but what should she say? She could not be sorry he was in trouble, when the trouble was so richly deserved. She could not bring herself to wish him well. She was aware that her email sounded as if she had not heard about his arrest, but rather that memories of him had stirred in her without prompting. That did not matter. Indeed it might be to the good. Perhaps he would be pleased by a version in which he was not incriminated, and perhaps she would receive what he remembered of Mark untrammelled by other matters. She pressed 'Send'.

~

Julia had a text from Tony: *Will be late. Will tell you why.*

Julia's reproductive cycle was on her mind. She had an ovulation calendar and an ovulation calculator, both elaborate; but Julia had a kind of mind and a spirit of perseverance equal to their complexities. She had been filling in the charts for several months already, with a view to being well prepared. She did not want to miss her moment.

Nevertheless she was mildly intrigued by Tony's text. There was a portentousness about 'Will tell you why', which struck a note she was not used to from him. So when she heard his key in the door, she went out to meet him. 'Well?' she said.

He dumped his bag and stood glowering. 'I've been with the police,' he said.

'What happened? Come and sit down.'

'Gerry Farrell reported to them that I had incited him to falsely accuse Father Pip. For compensation.'

Julia couldn't help laughing, and Tony's face relaxed into a smile. 'Ridiculous,' they said, together.

'As you know,' Tony went on, 'I rang Gerry to tell him about Father Rog. And that put it into his mind to accuse Father Pip. I never thought of that for a moment. Where is a phone hacker when you need one? Anyone who heard our conversations would know, actually, I was trying to stop him bringing Father Pip into it, the opposite of inciting.'

'Why did the police take it seriously?'

'They thought it was odd I phoned Gerry after all these years, and I admit it was. I couldn't deny that. It was when I was being a clerical abuse bore, and trying to think of people to tell who would be interested about Rog. I couldn't deny to the police that I never phone Gerry and he isn't a friend. So why did I do it then? So they were grilling me, and what upsets me is: what if they think I accused Rog so as to get compensation? That I'm running a racket. Or trying to.'

Julia made tea. Tony could see she was disposed to make light of his adventure, and this helped him hope it would not come to much.

'You're the same age as Gerry,' said Julia. 'Why ever would they suppose you had undue influence to exert? It's nonsense. It'll blow over.'

She was right as it turned out, though one of the reasons she was disposed to brush it aside was that she remembered she had not checked her vaginal discharge for stretchiness, and needed to hurry off to the loo, while Tony, still fulminating, began work.

It was sad for Julia that the flat was getting so nice, for she could not allow herself to love it. To allow herself to love it was to side with the career Julia, and not the Julia who needed quite different accommodation, possibly soon, to house her baby. So, however enchanting and intricate Tony's woodwork, Julia had to see her flat as an improving asset, rather than as her home. It was difficult.

Chapter 9

Romola's school was closed for the day. She would have gone on the demo herself, but she decided to seize the chance to be at the nursing home on a weekday morning, unusually, in case that timing gave her a better opportunity to talk to anyone in charge.

The nurse Romola thought of as the senior nurse, and whom she identified as a Virginia McKenna lookalike, was in the corridor outside Hereward's room. Romola went straight up to her.

'Excuse me,' she said, 'I can see you are busy. But I just want to know if there is any further news or bulletin on my brother.' At the word 'brother', for reasons she did not understand, tears came to the eyes of stoical Romola. She hoped the nurse would not notice, but she did, and looked sympathetic.

'We are monitoring him,' said the nurse. 'We are keeping a careful eye.'

'For signs of life?' Romola noticed the nurse's name badge said Sister Mandy Wall. Sister. So she had been right to assess her as senior.

'Yes, and for everything else. You have to face the fact that he is in a very deep coma, almost what is known as a vegetative state.'

'Almost? Please tell me, whatever truth you know.'

'Yes. We have a coma scale, and he is on number three, which is the worst, with the least good prognosis for recovery.'

'Recovery of any sort?'

'Yes.'

'But you do see, in the news, that someone who has been in

a coma for years comes round . . .' Romola broke off. She had to remove and wipe her glasses.

'It does happen, but only very, very occasionally. That's why it's recorded on the news, precisely because . . .'

'Have you ever seen it?'

'No.'

'So, with all your experience, what do you expect to happen to Hereward?'

'He could go on like this for a long time.'

'Years?'

'Unusual, but known.'

'And otherwise?'

'He is already having cardiac arrests. Since he's been here there've been three. One of them may carry him off, painlessly. Or he may just slip away.'

'If he was your brother, would you think that would be the best?'

'It's complicated, because of the remote chance that he may recover, though the recovery would be partial and limited. But the fact that he came through the operation, with the cerebral accident he had, testifies to his will-power. Will to live. From Mr Bleaney's notes, he is lucky to be alive.'

'Or unlucky.'

'Depending how you look at it. We've asked you this already, I know, but the fact is he did not leave a living will.'

'Saying "Do not resuscitate"? No, he didn't.'

'Exactly.' The nurse sympathised with Romola, and could tell she wanted her tears ignored. She knew Romola would not want a cup of tea. She liked Hereward, and was sorry for him. There were some patients you liked more than others, despite the remoteness of the states they were all in. She had started reading Hereward's novels.

'So we just wait,' said Romola. 'Perhaps at some level he knows when I am here. Who can tell?'

The nurse did not answer this for a full minute. She did not know what to say. Finally, 'There's a lot we don't understand. The monitors can tell us a great deal, and so can consultants, the many consultants who have seen him. But they can't tell us everything.'

So, again, Romola sat. Now that she had started crying, she couldn't stop. There are always plenty of tissues in the vicinity of hospital beds, and Romola took and used them. Nothing had been said that she did not already know, but she had not liked to hear the word 'vegetative', although she had to endure seeing it on google. She was sleeping badly, and this increased her uncharacteristic proclivity to tears. She had always been a good sleeper, rolling into bed exhausted from her day's work at half past eleven or twelve. When she woke up it was morning and she got up. Now she was experiencing for the first time the inordinate length of those seven hours when sleep is patchy or impossible. The will-power that it appeared she shared with Hereward was preventing her work from suffering. But she herself was suffering.

If Romola screwed up her tear-filled eyes, Hereward became a blur, although unmistakably Hereward; and she could manage not to see the tubes that came out of his nose, and the proximity of some of his machines. She did this for a while, to recreate the real Hereward. Then she wiped her eyes and looked at the day's batch of Get Well cards. Then she leant forward and, as she always did, said: 'Romola is here.' She touched his hands. They were warm and passive, as ever. She touched his face with the backs of her fingers. Cool and healthy. His face had filled out slightly, and seemed to have lost some of its deep lines. Or, rather, some of its lines were less deep. It's because there have been no expressions on his face, thought Romola. Before he dies his face will be quite smooth.

For Romola was beginning to believe that Hereward would die. Perhaps he would slip away, inconspicuously, between one machine-engendered breath and the next. Or perhaps there would be a cardiac arrest, probably in the night. The medical team would rush in and try everything. But he would be carried off, painlessly. Would he slip away, or would he be carried off? Either way, she would probably be telephoned too late.

Romola had watched for many hours, over the weeks, and seen no twitch in Hereward's face or finger. She no longer expected one, as, at the beginning, she had, from moment to moment. And yet, how wonderful it would be if it happened. And, according to the nurse, it could. It was not likely, it was an outside chance. But it could. Hereward had a will to live. His will to live could not be aiming at such a life as this.

She never liked leaving, but leave she did. There was a pile of A level essays, and she was glad of the extra hours afforded by the demo. Before she settled to her marking, she had a look at the inbox. There was a message from Hereward's publishers.

Dear Romola Tree,

This must be a terrible time for Hereward's family, and we are all very sorry.

We understand from Hereward that he has a completed novel in your charge. This makes us very happy. At your convenience, and we do understand that you and everyone else close to Hereward must be very stressed, perhaps you could send us an electronic copy, which Hereward informed us you would have access to.

We are all rooting for Hereward!

Romola had foreseen this moment. Now it was upon her.

She had read the untitled manuscript several times and now knew it quite well. She had two criticisms of it. One was the superabundant detail about dates and places important in the Risorgimento. Quite often – too often – the details seemed to have come loose from the plot and the characters, and to be there for their own sake. Pages at a time. Romola recognised the hand of the careful scribe of Hanulaland, with a back-story and back characters for every event. She was sure that this detracted from the interest of the novel. At one point, there was even, of all things, a conversation between two elderly Italian scholars, offering each other copious information about similar situations in Italian history. Not only was this dull in itself, at least, to

Romola; but also it was such an obvious device to purvey information while maintaining the frame of a novel. This chapter was Romola's most disliked, and she found the perfunctory attempts to offer the scholars characters, when in fact they were mouthpieces, almost funny. Romola did not want Hereward's last novel to be a flop. Her other objection was the ending. She found it too sad, too negative, too hopeless. That again was a difference between Hereward's mind and hers, well-remembered from Hanulaland days, but, in the present circumstances, not something she could easily bear.

A temptation for Romola was to tamper with Hereward's novel. This possibility had swept through her during a sleepless night, and she had been astonished by it. But there was no denying that it would be feasible. Only she, so far, had access to the text. If she made alterations, no one would ever know. It had the nature of a perfect crime. The only person who could know would be Hereward, returned to life and with his faculties intact. Otherwise, no one would ever know. The joy of Hereward's recovery, should it happen, would dwarf, or reduce to nothing, the awkwardness of confessing to him that she had taken it upon herself to be his editor. Hereward's recovery would make nothing else matter. But an awkwardness would remain, as would the fact that Romola had done something very wrong, which was not how she was used to Hereward seeing her. In contemplating doing something so displeasing to him, had she implicitly given up hope of his restoration to life? Was she assuming there could be no day of reckoning? Or was she, on the other hand, issuing a challenge to him: come back, come back now, or you will regret it, you will find your work appropriated, depredated, its meaning modified and distorted, under your name?

Neither of these motives reached the heart of her impulse. Sometimes, when Hereward was busy with something else, she had climbed to the attic by herself, and seen set out neatly, his and hers, the toys from which the Hanulaland characters and stories had evolved. It did not seem odd to Hereward and Romola that a one-eared rabbit with a cross stitch nose and what remained of a red jacket should be a brave and legendary hero, nor that a wooden duck should be his valiant lady. When Romola went up alone, she liked to move Hereward's figures, though etiquette did not allow either to handle the other's objects. She put them back in place before she left, of course; but there was a special pleasure, a transgressive pleasure, in fingering them as if they were her own. There was a small, stout teddy, who was always recumbent, because the great knight it stood for had been laid low by arrow wounds. This knight was carried on a litter to battlefields by two of his sons, who took their origins respectively from a clockwork mouse and a china hippo. Romola did not welcome Sir Flabodar's permanent disability, and in secret acts of defiance stood the teddy on its feet. Before she came downstairs she laid it flat again. Hereward need never know. What offered the special pleasure was having mastery of Hereward's creatures. Romola had the same pleasure now, when she thought that she could, if she wanted, tamper with Hereward's prose, and never be detected.

Romola sighed, and got down to her marking. It seemed that Hereward's publishers were content for her to be dilatory in her response. So that could wait. Having worked her way through the pile of scripts, she made sure she was abreast of tomorrow's lessons, and of a head of departments' meeting in the lunch hour. Afternoon turned to early evening. She heard Roger's key in the latch, and a minute later he put his head round the door.

'I've got fish,' he said. 'I'll do it with a bit of rice and peas. Is that all right? It'll be very quick.'

'Thank you, that's lovely,' said Romola, who never had to shop or cook these days.

They had a bottle of wine with supper. It was on Roger's mind that he must find a way of answering Betty's email. He would have liked to talk about it with Romola, but she didn't know, and mustn't know, about Mark.

'Was I a weird child?' he asked.

Romola looked at him, surprised by the question. She was well aware that she had not taken as much interest in his problems and his approaching prison sentence as she would have if

Hereward had not been ill. It was difficult to have two brothers in such deep trouble at the same time, and Hereward mattered so much more. And, of course, Hereward had not brought it on himself.

'You were so much younger than us.'

'Only five years younger than you, six years younger than Hereward.'

'That's an awful lot, when you're a child, obviously nothing now. I'm wondering if you were weird.'

'I've turned out weird, haven't I? With my sexual preferences.'

'You should have seen a therapist.'

'I have done a bit of that. When I asked to be moved from St Thorlac's because of Tony, obviously not giving the full details but indicating there had been an attraction, I had some treatment. Perhaps it did some good – I haven't offended since. But I think that's because I've been so careful. Specially about drink. I don't know.'

'I'm sorry I haven't been more help. It's been nice having you here. I'll miss you.'

'I'll miss you.'

'I'll come to see you in prison.'

'It might be miles away.'

'If it is, I'll only come once a week.' She smiled at him. These two had never been close, before this unexpected cohabitation. 'I don't remember you as weird. We thought you were clever. I don't remember us playing with you. You were always at such a different stage from us.'

'And you two were so close.'

'Sometimes I feel I have never in all my life loved anyone but Hereward,' said Romola, and the tears came back. 'That's a bad limitation, if true. Mind you, I'm using the word love in a very gold standard way. In a normal sense I love lots of people, including you.'

'I have thought I have never loved anyone.'

'Tony?'

'Well, obviously not gold standard. I can't have desired his welfare.'

'You loved Mum.'

'Does that count?'

They were both quiet, because they were not sure. But Romola's mind could not keep from Hereward for long, and she dabbed her eyes with one of the paper napkins which presbytery-trained Roger had introduced to the dining table, and said,' I can't bear it if Hereward dies, and I can't bear it if he lives, lives like this.'

'How was he today?' Roger knew this was a feeble question, and that it came from someone who did not really care about Hereward, but pretended to.

'An effigy of Hereward, as ever.' Romola knew he did not care.

'But warm.'

'I know.' Romola dabbed.

They had finished their very nice first course. Roger got up to fetch the fruit bowl, and embarked on an orange. 'What about Carina?' he said.

'Well, we must look after her, for Hereward's sake. Personally I find her a dreary little thing, you are better with her.'

'Her mother's coming over for the weekend.' At one moment it had looked as if Carina's mother might bring Alessandro, to give him a glimpse of London. This had been vetoed by his school, in the middle of term, and, learning this, Roger had felt a mixture of disappointment and relief, both intense.

Romola took in this quite interesting news, but felt too low to say anything but, 'Well, that'll save the phone bill.'

~

Julia was tense. She was trying not to be, in case calm favoured conception. All the auguries from her ovulation predictors stood fair, and her cervical mucus was profuse, clear and stretchable. More important, Stan and Vicky were on their way.

Julia already had a turkey baster, which she used in cooking sometimes, though more often to rescue over-watered plants from sitting in puddles. However, she did not think it pristine enough for her present purposes, and ordered one from John Lewis. She carefully washed and rinsed it. It was now balanced on a towel on the radiator in her bedroom, ready for action. A small soup bowl was on the shelf in the bathroom. With a view to speed, she was wearing no knickers under her summer skirt.

It crossed her mind from time to time that this was completely mad. Why did she want a baby? She scarcely knew. The main motive, which she had hammered out in her therapy, was that she did not want to be a person who had never had a baby. This did not seem a very good reason. It did not have enough to do with love, or another life. Yet it was formidably strong. Was this the right moment, and wouldn't it be better to wait until she had a man who could be the baby's father? By that time it would be too late. *Carpe diem*. But was this the *dies*? And with Stan's sperm? She didn't know. And, of course, it might well not work, despite the exemplary state of her cervical mucus. It was partly the fact that it seemed so far-fetched as a procreative act that spurred her determination to try. It was worth a try. If it had been sure to be a success, she might have drawn back. She would not have drawn back, though. She knew that. If she drew back now, when would circumstances be more favourable? Probably never. And she was running out of time. She did not want to turn forty with the situation unresolved.

She would have to take maternity leave. But a number of colleagues did that. Julia did not want to be part of the reason why most consultant posts go to men, and, so far in her career, she had been a model of punctiliousness. She hoped she could still be so. She was unlikely to apply for more than one maternity leave in her working life. Her situation was unusual, but this need not be broadcast. No one who was not an intimate, and Julia had few, would have to know that she was not in a relationship, and that she had scraped the barrel for sperm. Stan would be sure to want to put about his part in the story in what remained of their shared social circle. But that circle had nothing to do with the hospital. Would Vicky object to its being a matter for gossip? That could be imagined either way. So Julia mused.

Julia was not used to passionate desires. Her clear, practical character resisted them. The passion to have a baby, incurring, if fulfilled, influxes of untidiness and uncertainty in her orderly life, ran counter to the rest of herself. This was one of the reasons why her therapist looked kindly on it, while trying to appear unbiased. The last time Julia's therapist had seen Julia moved was when she fell briefly in love with Stan. That had not amounted to much. Her father's death was something she soldiered through, rather than underwent. She was moving towards having a baby, against all reason in terms of convenience and professional ambition, not just to avoid being left out of an important life experience, nor only to keep up with women who are seen to live full lives, but because, otherwise, she could die without having located her heart.

Julia opened a bottle of wine and put glasses out. She put out a few olives. Then she waited. She heard a car draw up outside, and then the doorbell.

'Delivery team arrives,' said Stan, smirking. The three of them went into the sitting room and sat down. Wine was poured. It was so like the start of an ordinary social occasion that for a moment Julia thought they might have changed their minds, and the concealed thud of misery she then experienced showed her how set she was on the enterprise, had she doubted. But all was well.

Vicky spoke first. 'We've decided to do it together,' she said. 'Stan and I will go into another room – is your bedroom a possibility, or a spare room? – and do the deed. Together. We felt better about it like that.'

'Good idea,' said Julia, disconcerted.

No one was very interested in their wine. Stan ate several olives. 'We came at once to your call,' he said. 'I am feeling quite hungry. I hope that does not have an adverse effect on fertility.'

Julia hoped embarrassment didn't. She picked up the bowl from the bathroom as she led them into her bedroom, not having a spare room. 'I'll put the bowl near the radiator,' she said. 'We don't want it too warm, but it shouldn't be cold, either.' She put the bowl beside the turkey baster.

'Blood heat,' said Vicky.

Julia withdrew, closing the door behind her. She returned to the sitting room. She had envisaged herself and Vicky chatting or giggling or both, at this point, but as it turned out she was on her own, feeling foolish and forlorn. She ate an olive. She could not help listening. She could hear muted guffaws and chuckles. After not very long she heard her bedroom door open and Vicky came into the sitting room, bearing the bowl, enacting a pantomime of hurry. Stan followed, also in burlesque mood. 'We have to rush,' said Vicky. 'The babysitter only had half an hour.'

Julia agreed that they should let themselves out. What might a blast from the front door do to the tepid fluid? She hurried into her bedroom, and by careful suction effected the transition from bowl to turkey baster. She lay down on her bed. The insertion seemed to go well. When she inspected the turkey baster, it was empty. She turned on the radio and lay still, allowing what was to happen to have its way.

~

Kim Ryan and Ayleen Brown were at the school gates. They claimed one of the children who poured out, many holding rolled-up pictures they had done during the day. The one who belonged to Kim and Ayleen wanted to show Kim his picture, which happened, although Ayleen was saying, 'When we get home, wait till we get home, Nan's coming home with us.' Then the children all ran ahead, and the women followed, Ayleen pushing a buggy with two smaller children.

'You remember Mark Winterborne?' said Kim.

'Of course, Mum. No one could forget. Why?'

'His mother has been on the phone a lot recently.' Kim had judged it better not to tell Ayleen about the newspaper reports of Roger Tree, and been relieved that Ayleen had not seen them. Why should Ayleen have to know? She was finding the church difficult enough without that.

Kim went on, 'Betty Winterborne is desperate for details about Mark. I just thought I'd tell you, in case you remember anything

I could pass on to her. It doesn't have to be about the school trip. It could be what he was like as a classmate. She wants anything.'

'Poor woman,' said Ayleen. She looked at the running figure of her own ten-year-old. 'Well, you know what he was like, yourself. Small. Very sweet. If we played in the toy house, he was always one of the children. I was the mum. He liked that game. He wasn't a great one for football.'

'Well, I'll pass that on to Betty. She will like that. Any memory.'

'Well, here's something not to pass on. The night of the school trip, he was really upset. He was crying and crying, in his sleeping bag. I crawled over to him. He was missing his mum, I think.'

'What a sad memory. When he would never see her again.'

'If I was Mrs Winterborne, and it was Kevin –' Ayleen looked again at the running back of her eldest – 'I think I would want to know that.'

'No point now, it's over twenty years ago.'

'I wonder. Poor woman.'

Chapter 10

A month passed. Some days, there was a hint of autumn in the air.

Betty worried that it had rained so little, and hosed her beautiful plants, still in full flower, and hosed even the lawn, love for it guiltily stronger than duty to conserve water. Every morning, as soon as she got up, she opened the door to the garden and looked out. She felt peace and satisfaction; peace because of the trustworthiness of Nature, satisfaction because of how justly she had cooperated with it. Sometimes, from the garden door, she would see a deadhead, and go out in her dressing gown. Something else would always detain her, a trailing frond, or a clematis strand that was groping. It was her world, but not a private one, for she loved people to see the garden.

Indoors, she was in the process of turning what had been Julia's room into a studio for herself. Although Mark's room was the larger, the room that had been Julia's was lighter. It was on the side of the house that got more sun, and it had responded well to a clear-out and the introduction of an easel. This was also Betty's world, but a more private version, in that she did not want Julia to think that she was becoming a scatty and dabbling old lady in a smock. She did have a smock, but she kept it out of eyeshot, in her studio.

It was a bit of a relief that Roger Tree had not answered her email. She dreaded disturbance in her life which had now become almost serene. The garden had helped, of course, and, as she knew, darker evenings would strain her capacities to be unmoved by her loneliness. But she was hopeful. Since she had gone back into her pain about Mark, and developed a keener interest in him as a person, she had become happier. She had gained a wondering self-esteem from finding the strength to hold and handle the hideous shifting shapes which her Proteus had assumed.

Julia had given her a Kindle for her birthday, and she found reading more enjoyable than usual, as there were bothers with her eyesight that did not seem to arise with the Kindle. She was reading biographies: Dickens, Harold Macmillan, St Francis. She always looked to the end of the book, for the death, and when acquainted with that, started from the beginning.

Kim Ryan had told her on the telephone that St Malachy's was looking for volunteers to help the slow readers. Betty was seriously thinking about offering herself, one morning a week. How strange it would be to go into St Malachy's again. It was a challenge.

～

Roger had indeed still not answered Betty's email. Nor had he written the letter to the parish of Our Lady of Calvary. He wrote emails and deleted them. He wrote more and kept them on draft. He never pressed 'send'. His hearing was two weeks away now, and he must write both before that day.

He entertained the possibility that he did not feel as bad as his circumstances warranted because, through thick and thin, he had kept the habit of half an hour's silent prayer every day. He also said the Office, morning and evening, rather sheepishly, for he was not a proper priest any more. But he had known lay people who said the Office, and he was so used to it that it was hard to give up. So for an hour a day he would withdraw to the spare room in which he slept, open the window wide, and sit quietly on the one chair. Prison, he thought, with its implication for him of solitary confinement, would not debar him from this hour.

At this time he had two interviews with a solicitor laid on for him by the diocese. She was a nice young woman, sympathetic, though unwavering in her disapproval of him. However, she expressed a hope that he might be eligible for an open prison. She was sifting through his material for mitigating circumstances which might shorten his sentence. The best she could see was there had been no evidence of further acts of abuse since 1995, though the police had investigated possible witnesses at Our Lady of Calvary; and that in other ways he had been an exemplary priest. He would not see his solicitor again till court, and his scalp prickled when she told him this.

The letter to the parish was hard, but the one to Betty was worse, because it implied consequences. What if she wanted to meet? What if she asked about Mark's last twenty-four hours? Would he feel compelled to tell the truth? If not the truth, what could he say? These thoughts revolved, causing panic and inertia. What was the right thing to do? What would a brave, good person do? What would Romola do? Was this his chance of a lifetime to do something good? For over twenty years, it had been pleasant for Roger, almost something to gloat over, to think that no one could ever know what had happened to Mark the night before he died. Now there was a part of him that did not want that cosiness. But if he told Mark's mother, which might be what a brave and good person would do, she would suffer. He would be unburdening himself at her expense. And what if she went to the police? Roger was terrified of what the press might say: 'Murderous secret of well-respected Catholic priest.'

One day he got on a coach and went to what had been the camp site by the river. There were shops there now, fronting on to the road the other side of the site. Disgraced by childhood death, the site had been obliterated for camping. It was difficult to find the right place. He walked the path beside the river, which was new, looking for the flat stone. It was there, unchanged amongst the many changes.

~

Romola too had an email still to write. In her case there was an attachment to append. That would be tackled when the rush of work abated. Meanwhile, she was still capable of imagining herself altering Hereward's manuscript.

She was pleased by the high estimate Roger had received for the rings. It would still be some time before the house would have to be put on the market. There were the pictures to go, yet. The watches, as expected, had only amounted to a few thousand pounds – three weeks, in terms of Hereward's maintenance at Mayton Road. It was strange that Hereward had adored rings, thought Romola, he who had never married. It was a pity the collection could not be kept together, as a wonder and curiosity, but no, the rings were to be auctioned singly.

The visit of Carina's mother came and went. She made the trip to England in the hopes of persuading Carina to come home. Carina was not ready for that. She wanted her mother to stay longer with her, but her mother could not be spared from the family. So they had an emotional reunion and a sad parting. Carina explained that she did not want to go home now, while Hereward might yet recover. She took her mother to visit Hereward. Carina's family had got on well with him, and had seen much of him in the previous year, which he had spent mostly in Italy. They had got on well with him, but on the other hand, he was fifty-six and Carina twenty-one. They had not thought it suitable. And now this had happened. Carina's parents wanted her back in Genoa, where she could forget Hereward, and make a life for herself with a nice young man; and if a letter arrived sometime in the future to say she was a rich woman, that would be very nice. But that might not be the way of it. Hereward's wealth might all drain away on his upkeep. Then what would happen? This was not Carina's mother's problem. She did wonder about it, however, that being her turn of mind, after meeting Romola and the Padre, neither of whom seemed rich.

'Medicine is too good, these days,' Carina's mother said to her husband that evening. 'I would not want that to happen to me, if I have a stroke. Death is better.'

∽

Julia had failed to conceive at the first attempt, but she and her allies were willing to persist. Her calculators, calendars and predictors were in apple-pie order, and again the phone call was made. Stan and Vicky arrived on the doorstep. Stan impersonated a pizza-deliverer, which to Vicky, who had had a few drinks, was hilarious. Julia did her best to find it fun. The known process was repeated exactly. This time Stan and Vicky could have stayed all evening, and there could have been a meal; but Julia had a bad cold and demurred.

A matter of days after this episode, Julia began to feel symptoms. Not only did she see them confirmed on the internet, but she also found them familiar from her previous pregnancy. She did a pregnancy test, and it was positive.

Chapter 11

It was the last paragraph of Hereward's book which bothered Romola. The book's geographical detail and historical ramifications, in which a non-skipping reader might become enmeshed and frustrated, were pure Hereward. That was the way his mind worked. Possibly he would have done something about the excess of this, had he been in a position to revise the manuscript. Perhaps that was at least part of what he meant by implying to Romola that the book was unfinished. On his head be it, thought Romola, if critics found long passages contrived, or disclosing an un-assimilated research interest.

This was the last paragraph:

Tonino limped up the stairs, the wound in his leg bleeding profusely. It bled so fast that he was slipping in his blood before he could get a foot on the next step. He gripped the bannister. The men who had come to kill his father had set the house alight, and hot gusts came up the stairwell to where Tonino struggled. He could hear his mother screaming angrily, and then there was the sound of another shot, which silenced her voice. Tonino reached the birdcage. Finula was uneasy, because of the noise, and the smoke that was now making its way upstairs. She was pleased to see Tonino, and hopped in the cage, making little noises and pressing her head against the bars in the hope of encountering his finger. Tonino looked at the wire loop which held the door of the cage shut. He hesitated. Then he tightened the loop, twisting the wire round and round so that there could be no possibility of escape. The floorboards were hot under his feet, and he jiggled from foot to foot. Then he fell.

Romola could not bear this. There had been moments in the book where it had looked as if there could be an ending – not happy, perhaps, but an ending in which the human spirit shows its strength. To Romola, the book needed such an ending, or what was the point of all the foregoing strife and courage? The loyalty and sacrifice? Tonino was a strong character throughout the novel, a resourceful and intrepid member of the group, though too young to be allowed to carry arms. Romola had been surprised and impressed by Hereward's ability to make a child real. Tonino's only link with a more normal childhood, throughout, had been his pet bird. And then Tonino came to this, and on this note the novel ended. Romola cried, stamped her foot, and could not bear it.

She was well aware that to interfere with another person's work was a terrible thing to do. Especially when he would never be able to expostulate and expound. Whatever Hereward meant by that terrible ending, he meant it. Whether at a personal level about a child, or in a wider context about societies, or as an unconscious prophecy of his own doom, he meant it. He would have been working up to this moment. A happier ending devised by Romola would steal his message from him, and utterly contradict whatever it was that he had tried to say.

With thoughts like these, she postponed answering the publishers' email.

It was a busy time of year for Romola, even if she hadn't been rushing to Hereward's bedside most days after school. She was on various committees which chose future syllabuses. What was on the English syllabus was a matter Romola took very seriously, because some pupils might never read books after A level. She was keen to get *Mansfield Park* as an A level text. Previously she had rooted successfully for *Emma*. Early Jane Austen had been staples of syllabuses for years, but not the later three, which, to Romola, were the much more important. There was a consensus that the name 'Fanny', in 'Fanny Price', was an insuperable problem. The worst moment came with Henry Crawford's words: 'It is Fanny that I think of all day, and dream of all night'. No class of teenagers could stand up to that. An edition for schools had been mooted, cutting out that sentence. Romola thought it would be safer to remove the entire difficulty by changing 'Fanny' to 'Annie'. Romola's views were always strong, and younger committee members regarded her as something of a termagant. However, she remained on the committee, knowing she was not welcome, and although the second half of the summer term, bringing with it revision leave and exams, could have been restful.

One day, she read Hereward the last paragraph of his book, and then the last paragraph with an emendation she had in mind. She read them loud and clear, having explained why she was doing so, with one eye to the door of his room, in case a member of staff or another visitor should make a sudden appearance, and wonder. There was no flicker from Hereward. She had not expected one, but after she had done that, she was a couple of inches nearer to making her alteration.

'I often hear you speaking to him,' said Sister Mandy Wall. 'Distantly, I mean, not the words. It is very touching.'

'You mean because it is so hopeless?' These two women knew each other better now, and Mandy was still ploughing respectfully through Hereward's novels.

'Because it's natural. His fiancée also speaks to him.'

'Poor child.'

'I know!' They were both older women, and had moments when the phenomenon of Carina made them complicit about the vagaries of romance. They both felt they had a certain knowledge of life, but, when it came to Hereward's condition, the nurse held all the cards.

'Any change at all?' asked Romola. She knew it was tedious.

'I'm afraid not. He is actually doing quite well. He is not deteriorating, as people sometimes do in this state. May I ask if there are financial considerations?'

'Not yet. Eventually there will be. But not yet.'

Sister Mandy Wall looked at Romola. 'I don't think I've ever asked you if you would like counselling.'

'No, I wouldn't.'

'I thought not.' They enjoyed a moment of a different complicity.

There was a pause, then Romola asked, 'What do you mean by deteriorating?'

'I mean none of his major organs, except, of course, his heart, and you know about his brain. None of his organs – liver, kidney, digestion and so on – are out of action.'

'So if he came round, there would be no serious . . .' Romola couldn't think of a word for what she meant.

'Except the brain, of course. And the heart would remain vulnerable.'

'He should never have had that operation. He was fine, limping about.'

'He must have been in considerable pain, and his breathing was inhibited. I've looked at the hospital notes.'

'Better pain and inhibited breathing than this.'

'Yes. But who knew? His chances were very reasonable. There is always danger. Calculated risk.'

'He should have accepted the state he was in,' said Romola.

'He could have had a fatal heart attack at any moment.'

'He could have a cardiac arrest at any moment, now.'

Mandy had to go. She and Romola often faced a stalemate. She was sorry for Romola. She liked her. She herself had a Living Will securely lodged with her G.P.

～

'Hereward OK?' asked Roger, stupidly, as he served the pasta.

Romola did not answer. After a few mouthfuls, she said, 'I will miss your lovely cooking, Rog. Indeed, I shall miss you.'

'It's awful for you. Both your brothers. You will be all right, won't you?'

'Yes. I shall be visiting both of you, in your institutions. It's lucky we don't have to pay for yours.'

～

The next day Roger sat down at Hereward's computer and composed a letter to the parish. Before he could find it too flowery, too floridly contrite, too self-obsessed, too literary, too worm-like, too self-pitying, too self-justifying, or any of the other faults of which he accused his attempts, he pressed 'send'.

Then he wrote to Mrs Winterborne.

Dear Mrs Winterborne,

I am sorry to hear of the death of your husband, whom I remember well.

As to memories of Mark, he was a sweet and clever child. I did not have much to do with him. Roger deleted the last word and substituted: *his form at St Malachy's. He always seemed full of life. He liked the school trip, as many children always did, and he may have been over-excited, when he decided to make that dangerous jump. Memories fade over twenty years, but I still remember him well, and am very sorry for your tragic loss. If you would like to meet me, please feel free to make a suggestion.*

Yours sincerely
Roger Tree

Ghastly, but he couldn't do any better, and he pressed 'send'. To offer the possibility of a meeting was almost beyond what he could nerve himself to do, but he was glad he had done it. She would probably not take him up, after this vague and formal response; and anyway, if she did, he would probably be in prison, and what would happen to an email then, he had no idea, while a meeting would take on quite a different complexion.

~

Betty, however, was content when she read this. To her, its tone did not seem vague and formal, but engaged; and she was grateful that he mentioned the school trip, and indicated that Mark had been in high spirits. She walked with a lighter step that afternoon. The email left her with no wish to meet Roger, and she thought it nice of him to ask. Anyway, surely he must be in prison by now, and she could hardly visit him there.

The phone rang, and, surprisingly, it was Julia. She did not usually telephone until evening, when she finished work.

'Surprising time to ring, darling,' said Betty, who was in her studio.

'Yes, I know. Can I come round this evening? There's something I want to talk about.'

'Yes, of course, how lovely.'

~

Julia was happy. If, for half a second, she forgot the huge new thing in her life, bodily sensations of excitement reminded her, and she found and grasped what gave rise to them, and rejoiced afresh. She was triumphant, as one who has overcome obstacles, and come out the winner. She did not use the word triumphant to her therapist, for triumph has a bad press. She preferred the word empowered, which was also accurate. Another feeling was relief. The fear of being forever a childless woman was removed. It had been a depressing fear, and it was on its way to being gone. It was not quite gone, because of the possibility of miscarriage. She knew how to minimise the dangers of this, and how to keep herself in good health.

She tried to concentrate on work, but the thrills of excitement and empowerment that ran through her like electricity made her lose track, sometimes, of what her patients were telling her. She had to ask questions twice – 'and when did you first notice this lesion?' She wondered whether anyone could tell that she was different. Certainly Tony, who had nearly finished the job, did not seem to. She found herself smiling. When she looked in the mirror, there was the smile.

There were drawbacks. Once she was sure the pregnancy was established, she would have to move in with her mother. That would be soon. She was not sure how she felt about this. The alternative would be to make the move after the baby was born. This was less attractive. There would be enough to do, with a new baby, without moving house at the same time.

Paradoxically, it was foreign to Julia to be thinking about a baby. In all the time that a baby had been how she named her desire, the core of the longing had not been for the actual neonate. She did not know many babies, nor wish to, and was not a person to be enraptured by those of friends. Toddlers she found irritating. What had magnetised her, in the recent years of longing and enforced postponement, was the achievement. She felt that in her case, the organs which can only come into their own in pregnancy and childbirth had waited too long. Waste distressed Julia. Ovulation after ovulation had ripened, hoped, and despaired, while she went about her business, reaching goals in her career. Period after period had rinsed hope away; and patiently set up the next possibility. But all this activity would peter out before long, as Julia approached her fifth decade; and if she wanted to realise that immense potential, it must be now. Julia's motive was not the baby, crying on the end of the umbilical cord; her motive was herself, exonerated of childlessness, gynaecologically fulfilled, and able to hold her head up as a woman. But now that she was pregnant, she began to think about a baby. She had to. There were plans to be made. She found herself stopping in front of shops that sold prams. She looked up slings on the internet. She discussed breast-feeding with an antenatal nurse. The physical baby was taking shape in her mind, and while that little entity was not the main advantage of the enterprise she had set up for herself, she committed herself to it with duty and good will. It would have been nonsense not to.

As it penetrated her thoughts that a baby is a baby, she wondered about the gender of her own, which the ultrasound scan would determine. She also, for the first time, thought about the birth, and had qualms. She had shied away from a specialisa-tion in obstetrics, which seemed to be on offer at one time in her training, because difficult deliveries were too hair-raising. Errors could be fatal. Dermatology offered more time to make decisions. Also, again for the first time, it occurred to her that her baby might not be normal. She looked up statistics. She tried not to worry.

She decided not to tell friends yet, in case of mishaps. She would tell them when she was sure. She told Stan and Vicky, and Stan crowed at his fecundity.

And now she had to tell her mother.

'Guess what,' she said. 'Three guesses.'

'You're a consultant,' ventured Betty.

'Two more.'

'A new man?'

'One to go.'

Suddenly it was obvious. 'A baby?'

Julia beamed and nodded.

'Darling! How too wonderful!' This is what Betty said, as what else could she say? But her thoughts were rushing everywhere. Whose baby? She had better not ask, if Julia did not choose to say. What sort of affair had given life to this baby, if there was no new man? Wiser not to ask that either. Betty did not want to spoil the moment, but, for her, it was not the perfect moment Julia's face announced.

'It's only just happened,' said Julia, 'so I suppose I shouldn't be too sure. But somehow I am. That's why I'm telling you, though it's as early as can be.'

'My goodness,' said Betty, wishing she could say something better. 'However will you manage?' was another question not to ask, and Betty did not ask it.

But this Julia was ready to tell her, unasked. 'I shall have to move back home,' she said. 'You can be a proper grandmother. I'll put my flat on the market. Of course that is a wrench, but it's the only way. It's so lucky this is a perfect house and garden for a child.'

'My goodness,' said Betty. A year ago this would have been an answer to prayer. Now the word 'wrench' had resonated for her as well.

Julia suddenly thought Betty looked rather old. After a minute, she said, 'I'll tell you what. Even with me having my old room and the baby eventually having Mark's room, there is still the attic bedroom, and we could have an au pair. I will have money, from selling my flat. We will be able to afford help. You can practise your French or Spanish again, with a nice au pair. You can see it'll work!'

'Yes,' said Betty, 'I can see it'll work.'

If Julia was disappointed that Betty was not ecstatic, that disappointment remained under the surface of Julia's mind. It was too unexpected and too inconvenient to take notice of.

And Julia was right to suppose that there was a large part of Betty which was glad of the news. What Julia did not know about, and did not want to know, was the part of Betty to which the news was unwelcome. Left alone, Betty sat with her hands folded on her lap, thinking, and unable to rejoice. Her engagement with her loneliness had taken a great deal of energy and courage. Proteus had changed shape often, and, despite pain and terror, she had hung on. Now he was ready to tell her the truth, and the truth was that she was able to be alone. And now, already, that hard-won, barely tried capacity was to be taken from her.

Amongst her feelings was a cowardly relief. She was like a soldier who does bravely on the battlefield, and, before the battle is over, peace is declared. Within this declaration, she also heard the call of duty. In view of Julia's work, Julia couldn't possibly bring up her baby on her own. How providential it must seem to Julia, to have an idle, bereaved mother, ripe to be involved afresh in family life, longing to be a grandmother like her friends, alone in a house which was every inch a family house. Betty recognised this version of herself. But it was no longer the only one to be recognised. The studio would have to go. It had better go before Julia realised it existed, in case it made Julia guilty. The quiet evenings, brooding over Mark, would be no more. The sense that at last she could bear to be a person in her own right would not be put to the proof.

But, albeit unproved, it was there. Whatever it was that had grown and knitted within Betty in the last months need not unravel; perhaps could not. No one would know or notice, but she would remain true to it. She would conceal that she was deprived of what would have happened next, if she had been let be.

She tried to set herself to one side, and began to think about

Julia. Perhaps more of the story would come out, but at this point all was mystery to Betty. She had become used to being in awe of Julia, seeing a Julia who was unafraid of the real world, undaunted by being a single woman. But to manage a pregnancy by returning to mother and the parental house did not smack of enterprise and autonomy. That was mysterious, as was the provenance of the baby. Betty had not known Julia wanted a child. How long had this desire been going on? Betty had no idea. Or was the pregnancy a mistake, courageously accepted?

You don't necessarily know the people you love, thought Betty. Now it occurred to her that an unformulated understanding of this proposition had motivated her, recently, to research the life and death of Mark. She loved Mark. But had she set herself to know him? Of course she had not. There he had been, and she had known him as a cat knows its kitten. And it was the same with Julia, though different, in that there was a chance to get to know the adult Julia. In honesty, Betty did not warm to the task before her. Julia's takeover of the family house flustered and annoyed her, though no doubt Julia had every right, and Betty was pretty sure the plan would have appealed to Jack. Of course the baby would be adorable, but Betty did not want to live with a baby. 'You can be a proper grandmother,' Julia had said. Betty would not be a proper grandmother. She would be forever debarred from that experience. Instead, she would be a second mother.

She had better get any resentment out of her system now, she thought, for Julia must not see it. The poor girl would have enough to cope with without feeling unsupported by her mum.

Chapter 12

'What have you said to Carina?' Romola asked Roger. The hearing was tomorrow morning.

'She thinks I'm a missionary, and I'm being called somewhere top secret overseas.' Roger tried to elicit a glint of amusement from Romola about this version, but failed.

After a pause for thought, Romola said, 'Rog, you must tell her the truth.'

'Why? It would only upset her.'

'What if she sees something in the paper?'

'She never reads papers, or watches the news.'

'Things do get out. They always do. But that's not the only reason. How can you leave her with an idealised you when the truth is so far off? Anyway, she might like to come and visit you in prison. She's very fond of you, you know. She was telling me you are the only person who understands her.'

'You may be right. I haven't thought it through. If she did get wind, I would seem to have betrayed her by my lie.'

'You'd better pop over and see her after supper.'

Roger knew Romola was right. It reminded him of when she had made him, a little boy of five, take the Kit-Kat bars he had lifted back to the shop. Hereward had sided with her, of course. Roger disliked and resented her, now, as he had then; but he knew she was right.

After supper Roger set forth, in the warm evening of early autumn. He would not do this familiar walk again. He shivered. He had understood from the solicitor that he would go to a special wing for sexual offenders, probably in one of the London prisons. So he was more likely to be raped than to have hot soup poured down his shirt front. What a terrible mess he had made of his life.

It was difficult to tell Carina the truth. She was delighted to see him, having understood that they had already said their goodbyes. Perhaps because of the delight, and perhaps because she did not have the need to idealise him that Roger attributed to her, she took the news calmly. Indeed she was interested. For one thing, it provided the answer to the puzzle of why he had never been attracted to her. She was censorious, however, and said, sadly, that he deserved prison, and that people should suffer for their crimes. She said that the victim – unnamed, of course, by Roger – would probably suffer all his life, and maybe was doomed to be gay. She asked if he would like her to come to the hearing tomorrow, so that he could see the face of someone who loved him. He was touched, but said no. They had another goodbye, and he walked back to Romola's, now through twilight. It was a precious walk, and he said goodbye to it.

Everything was goodbyes. Romola and he had eaten their last supper together. The coming night would be his last in Romola's spare bedroom.

'Shall I help you pack?' said Romola.

'No. I can manage. I've hardly got anything.' He went to his room.

Romola thought about Roger. Because of Hereward, and to a lesser degree because of work, she had not sat down to think about Roger. Now she did, and felt sad for him. She looked back over his life, insofar as she knew it. He had been very much the youngest, left out of her and Hereward's passionate companionship, wailing to mum that they would not play with him. Mum, an elder daughter herself, was sympathetic, but identified with the big ones, and their right to privacy.

Over one of their many suppers, Roger and Romola had this conversation:

'Mum always sided with you two,' Roger said.

'But she adored you.'

'Did she? I adored her. Dad only loved you two.'

'Dad only loved Hereward.'

And now it was prison, for Roger. Romola supposed and hoped that he had enjoyed some happiness. He was enthralled by the Christian faith as an adolescent; did well at Oxford, with an RC circle of friends; never seemed to fall in love; was joyful about his vocation to the celibate priesthood, in which, as a career, at least, he had been successful, albeit no star. And now this. Now he was packing for prison. If it hadn't been for Hereward, thought Romola, she would have had more emotional energy to expend on Roger in the past months. She had not had that energy to spare, and it was too late now.

She knocked, and put her head round his door. He was in the chair, the window wide open, the light not on.

'I just want to say,' she said, and her voice cracked, 'that I think you have been very brave.'

'Thank you,' he said. 'And I want to say thank you for having me.'

And, indeed, where would he have gone, but for her? Romola did not like to think. Where did these priests go, when on bail? She would be at the hearing with Roger tomorrow. School term had not yet started, though it was imminent.

Roger's last night at Romola's was not as bad as his first. The element of shock had long since evaporated. He had become accustomed to his diminished life, and, in a way, it had been pleasant. His prison life would, of course, be a life further diminished; but he had borne the intermediate stage, and would bear the worst. Knowing Carina had been a mild joy. Working with Sotheby's over the stones, the rings and the watches had made him feel useful. Romola would have to manage the pictures herself, and possibly the house, depending on the length of his sentence, and, indeed, on the length of Hereward's. It had been fun to cook meals for busy Romola. He had enjoyed choosing and buying food, an activity which was new to him. Grief still gripped his heart, but anxiety no longer churned his guts.

He was pleased not to have heard from Betty Winterborne. At first, the suspense had been terrible. Then it had passed, turning into relief. He had made an honourable effort, he felt, and had braced himself for a meeting. But he had been spared. It seemed wrong that his prison sentence would be shorter than he deserved; but he had reconciled himself to this. He had offered Fate a chance, and Fate had not taken it. It now seemed certain that what had happened with Mark would never be disinterred.

He slept a little, and rose early. He found Romola already up.

'Hangman's breakfast,' said Romola. 'The first time I've cooked since you arrived.' She was in the kitchen, busy, warm, her hair untidy, a spatula in her hand, doing bacon and eggs.

'Your key and Hereward's,' said Roger, putting them on the table.

~

They set forth for the Crown Court together, but had to separate with a fumbled, public kiss. She made her way to the gallery, and took a seat in the front row, where a young man was already ensconced. The proceedings began. Romola learned more than she wanted to know about Roger's predation of Tony Tremlow, and her anger with Roger resurfaced. Roger was given three years. He deserves more, thought Romola, feeling on the floor for her bag, but I'm glad he's not getting more.

As Roger was led away, his eyes sought the balcony, and he waved. Both Romola and the man beside her waved back. 'Cheeky bastard,' she heard the man mutter.

'Why do you say that?' Romola asked him.

'He had the nerve to wave to me.'

'No. The wave was intended for me, his sister.'

Tony Tremlow went pink, embarrassed at his mistake, and also at the fact that there were tears in Romola's eyes.

'I am Romola Tree,' said Romola. 'And you are?'

Tony made himself known, and said he was the boy who had been assaulted.

'I'm so sorry,' said Romola. 'May I ask why you waved back?'

'I thought he was waving to me.'

'I know. But why did you wave back, if you thought he was being a cheeky bastard, waving to you?'

'I don't know why. Obviously he wouldn't have recognised me, after all these years. So I don't know why I thought the wave was for me. Or why I waved back.'

～

Julia remembered this stage of pregnancy from last time. She had not remembered it in the intervening years, but now it came back to her. She had not vomited so far, but was queasy, and had intense preferences for some foods over others. She thought about food much more than usual, and ate less. The muesli she habitually had for breakfast was anathema. Even the thought of it made her salivate with nausea. What she wanted was salami on buttered toast. So she had two pieces of that, with a cup of peppermint tea, coffee being unbearable even in imagination. Her sense of smell became more acute and very intolerant. She had to put her iron casserole away on a high shelf, in case an aroma of metal mixed with the stewed food the metal had absorbed over years assailed her. She had not got far enough in her first pregnancy to be confident that this phase would pass. Friends, and her pregnancy book, said it would. Physical discomfort eroded the euphoria, but not the satisfaction.

She was not blind to the possibility that she was riding roughshod over Betty, and this qualm became a topic in her therapy. After Jack's death, Julia had seen Betty lonely and lost, growing almost eccentric, with all those unnecessary visits to Sainsbury's, and daytime TV likely to be on. Julia had not been surprised, for she knew Betty quite well, and had a sense of Betty's vulnerabilities. She had worried about her. She had worried about Betty's future. She had worried about herself as

Betty's only remaining family member and only source of security. She must try to look after Betty, while keeping a certain distance, and holding on to a life of her own. That stance would have persisted, except for her need for a baby, and Betty's vital role in that project. It had not occurred to Julia that Betty would view this role as anything but a godsend. It seemed obvious, and obvious to Betty's friends, as well as to Julia, that what Betty would thrive on was to feel needed again.

Julia knew Betty had accepted her plan, but what she missed in her mother was joy. Betty gave the impression of a person who has knuckled down, rather than a person who has gained her heart's desire. This was upsetting for Julia. She felt cheated of her own munificence, and of Betty's gratitude. It was she, Julia, who was unexpectedly the needy one, and Betty the provider. Julia had foreseen the deal quite the other way round. She hoped the balance would be restored, when Betty saw and held the baby. She was sure of this, and had some grounds for her certainty.

So, as the two of them took the first steps towards the new arrangement, each had a secret. Betty's secret was that she would have liked to go on living alone. Julia's secret was that she had an inkling of this. Thus Julia knew Betty's secret, and Betty did not know Julia's. Each decided to behave as if her secret did not exist. This put a strain on the relationship.

'I was thinking,' said Julia, 'What if I have my old bedroom, and the baby can have Mark's? Mark's is bigger, and will be good for the baby's things.'

'The baby will be in with you, of course, at first,' said Betty.

Julia did not quite like this assumption of knowing better. 'Obviously,' she said. 'I'm thinking long term.'

'Yes, that's fine.'

'That still leaves the attic for a possible au pair.'

'I don't think we'll need an au pair.' Betty dreaded the prospect of coping with a homesick stranger.

Julia considered.

Betty went on, 'Do you see yourself breast-feeding? I hope so. But what about when you are at work, which is most of the day?'

Julia considered again. There seemed to be a lot of detail. 'I'm sure we'll manage,' she said. 'I'll have maternity leave at first. Then after that I could always express some milk in the morning, which would be there for feeds in the day. Lots of people do that. I won't have to leave for work in the morning until nine, and there'll be time before that. Then there'll be the weekends, and leave.'

'I'm not sure you could express enough for several feeds,' said Betty. 'A lot depends on the baby's appetite. All babies are different. Perhaps the baby had better be weaned at the end of your maternity leave.'

Again, Betty was showing she knew about babies. Julia fumed, and wanted an egg and cress sandwich. 'We don't have to think everything out now,' she said.

'OK,' said Betty, knowing Julia was annoyed.

'Let's go up and have a look at my bedroom and Mark's,' said Julia, 'with a view to this. You'll probably be happy to have them lived in again.' There was the hint of a question in Julia's voice, but only a hint. She did not want to betray her secret.

'I certainly will,' said Betty.

'My room looks pretty bare,' Julia remarked. 'I'm sure it had . . . Where's the chest of drawers?'

'In the cellar,' said Betty. 'We can easily get it up again.'

'Why ever did you . . . Oh, well, never mind.'

'I carried it down with the cleaner. She'll be here on Tuesday and we'll bring it up again. You mustn't, you know, heavy things . . .' Betty's sentence ended there.

Julia noticed that Mark's room, unlike hers, was as she remembered it. 'It's all very convenient, isn't it?' she said. 'The bathroom just next door.'

'Yes, it will work well. When Jack and I bought the house, we thought it would be right for children.' Betty liked to mention Jack, for she was convinced he would have been enthusiastic about Julia's homecoming.

'Dad would like this idea,' said Julia.

'I know,' said Betty.

Julia was not quite pleased with this. Did 'I know' show that Betty had thought this already, and needed to improve her own zest by imagining dad's? Now Julia was wondering whether to tell Betty about the child's fathering. Perhaps knowing that would enable Betty to feel more involved. One difficulty was that Betty disliked Stan. She had not always disliked him. It had started when Stan made a terrible fuss about Julia's attachment to her dying father. Julia did not want to mention Stan. She was happy to let Betty suppose she had been having an affair – perhaps not serious, perhaps more with an eye to pregnancy than anything else. That would be all right.

'You never mention a father for the baby,' said Betty, more pluckily than Julia knew.

'He won't be part of this,' Julia decided to say.

Betty thought of Jack, and how entirely he had been part of everything. She decided not to say, 'I can't imagine bringing up a child without its father. Sorry, darling, I know it happens all the time these days.' What she did say was, 'That seems rather sad.'

Because Julia agreed, this quiet remark irritated her. She was feeling rather sick. The faintly musty smell of Mark's bedroom did not agree with her. She no longer wanted an egg and cress sandwich. She fancied a plum, a large, bursting, sun-warmed Victoria plum, with a little strip of gum clinging to the outside. Possibly two. 'It's no good being sad,' she said.

'No, I know, and I'm not,' said Betty. 'You will tell me anything you want me to know as and when you feel like it. It's natural I should wonder.'

'Thanks for being so tolerant,' said Julia, with an effort. 'You know things are often complicated.' She wished she wanted to give her mother a hug, but she did not.

'Let's go downstairs,' said Betty, 'and have a nice drink together. I've got some wine.'

'Drink? I can't drink.'

'Oh, no, of course not.'

Chapter 13

It was the first day of the school term, indeed of the school year. Only the Year Sevens were in and, uniformed, solemn and good, had been, as the phrase went, 'inducted'. Everybody else would arrive tomorrow.

Romola went to Mayton Road after school. Then she came home. She was missing Roger more than she expected. There was no 'Hello!' from the kitchen, no smell of cooking. There was no one to wonder in vain how Hereward was, or to ask her about her day. The house was quiet and empty, unstirred by a second presence. It was chilly. On a day like this, Roger would have put a little bit of heating on, to greet her. Most of all, she missed seeing him. She missed his tall, lean figure, the same build as Hereward; his slow, rather uncertain movements; his smile.

She went to her computer to see if there was an email from him. Indeed there was.

I am in what they call a 'nonce wing'. It means a wing for sexual offenders. Acronym? You will think of one straight off. I have a room of my own, for the moment, which I never expected. So things are not too bad. I gather I won't be here for long. I am probably going to an Open Prison. Given what things might have been like, they are not bad. And from today I am allowed to email, which is great. You have to queue for the computers, and an officer can look at what I write if he likes, but what does that matter? I'm unlikely to say anything controversial. I wonder how the first day of the school year went. I hope you didn't forget to eat the rest of the shepherd's pie. There followed the name and address of the prison — *in case you want to visit me. The visiting hours are 2-4 some weekdays, that won't suit you; and more at weekends. I haven't got weekend details, but the 2-4 slot should be OK Sat. or Sun. An Etonian known as Gandalf and a Trinidadian called Jarry (I think) are both interested in me being a priest. Must stop — queue mounting up. Love, Rog.*

Romola was smiling when she finished reading this. All the news was as good as it could be, in the circumstances; and there was a jaunty quality, from 'Acronym?' on, that made her say to herself, knowing it was an exaggeration, 'Trust Rog to fall on his feet!' She continued to smile as she microwaved what was left of the shepherd's pie.

It had always been her intention to deal with the matter of Hereward's manuscript before the beginning of term. She had not done so, and, over the summer, Hereward's publisher had nudged her twice. She decided that tonight must be the moment. Tomorrow she would be caught up in the new school year, she would bring work home; she would be up to her eyes.

The question was whether to send the attachment to Hereward's publisher as it was, or to change it. Her temptation to tamper had narrowed down to the wish to change the last paragraph. She turned it up on the computer.

Tonino limped up the stairs, the wound in his leg bleeding profusely. It bled so fast that he was slipping in his blood before he could get a foot on the next step. He gripped the bannister. The men who had come to kill his father had set the house alight, and hot gusts came up the stairwell to where Tonino struggled. He could hear his mother screaming angrily, and then there was the sound of another shot, which silenced her voice. Tonino reached the birdcage. Finula was uneasy, because of the noise, and the smoke that was now making its way upstairs. She was pleased to see Tonino, and hopped in the cage, making little noises, and pressing her head against the bars in the hope of encountering his finger. Tonino looked at the wire loop which held the door of the cage shut. He hesitated. Then he tightened the loop, twisting the wire round and round so that there could be no possibility of escape. The floorboards were hot under his feet, and he jiggled from foot to foot. Then he fell.

She had read this paragraph until she nearly knew it by heart, and now she read it again, several times. She sat back in her chair, and thought.

The Resistenza group which meant everything to Tonino had been defeated. His parents and friends were dead or dying. He himself was mortally wounded. No hope was left. It was only in the matter of the bird that he could make a personal choice. And Tonino inflicted cruel destruction on the bird he loved. Tonino's short life had not offered him choices. From birth, he was swept into a political movement in which, locally, his parents were pivotal and his house a focus. Now a choice presented itself to him. And this was how Hereward wanted him to exercise that choice.

So Hereward's message was – was it? – that we can't rise above what has happened to us, in order to make something better happen to what we love. This struck Romola as not only unacceptable, but untrue. But, when all was said, it was what Hereward had written. It was only by accident that his manuscript had fallen into her busy-body hands before it fell into the publisher's reverential ones. But was this paragraph, perhaps, precisely the one that Hereward had hoped to rethink? If so, Romola had every right to rethink it for him. But this she did not believe, attractive though the idea was. Probably, if she knew Hereward, what he wanted was to add more details – names, places, dates, – with the like of which the book was already overloaded. The message of the last paragraph was the core of the book. It must have been in Hereward's mind all along, and, indeed, accounted for the introduction into the story of the pet bird.

Romola cut and pasted the paragraph. She deleted two of Hereward's sentences, and interpolated her own. It read as follows:

Tonino limped up the stairs, the wound in his leg bleeding profusely. It bled so fast that he was slipping in his blood before he could get a foot on the next step. He gripped the bannister. The men who had come to kill his father had set the house alight, and hot gusts came up the stairwell to where Tonino struggled. He could hear his mother screaming angrily, and then there was the sound of another shot, which silenced her voice. Tonino reached the birdcage. Finula was uneasy, because of the noise, and the smoke that was now making its way upstairs. She was pleased to see Tonino, and hopped in the cage, making little noises and pressing her head against the bars in the hope of encountering his finger. Tonino looked at the wire loop which held the door of the cage shut. Then he loosened the loop, prising it open until it tinkled on the floor. He opened the door, and stepped back. Finula hopped up to stand on the threshold of the cage. She looked around, and then she flew. She flew straight out of the window, up and up, and disappeared into the blue sky. Tonino watched her, then watched the patch of sky into which she had disappeared. The floorboards were hot under his feet, and he jiggled from foot to foot. Then he fell.

Romola cut and pasted this paragraph into the manuscript, obliterating Hereward's. She was set on her course, and nothing would stop her now. No one could ever find out what she had done. She forwarded the novel to the publisher's email address, and pressed: 'send'.

～

Carina was someone else who missed Roger. Not to have his key in the door, his quiet, diffident presence was a privation in an existence already sparse. She also missed him as someone she could admire. She thought with regret about his crime.

Not getting up until lunch time took care of the mornings, but that left the rest of the day. She had her English class two afternoons a week, and she had made two friends, with whom she went shopping, and, occasionally, to films. She could not go shopping too often because of money. She did not want to overspend her allowance, particularly now that she would have to answer directly to Romola. She thought of going to a gym, to cope with the fact that she was putting on weight. She had not got around to finding one. Sometimes she went for walks in the streets, or very occasionally on Hampstead Heath, in the failing light of the September evenings, and wished she was in Genoa. She thought about her friends, and what they might be doing at this moment, at home. When she got in, she sometimes emailed them. She did not telephone them, or not on the landline, because Romola had sighed and gone silent when the phone bill arrived. Romola said she could ring her mother as much as she liked, but perhaps, sometimes, she could wait until after six, or sometimes her mother might ring her. Romola did not have to say much for Carina to feel rebuked. She was still afraid of Romola, but less so since her mother's visit, when she had seen her mother and Romola sitting down together over a cup of coffee, and poor Romola practising her ridiculous Italian. Several times a week Carina visited Hereward. Her visits were getting briefer. There was no one to talk to, and nothing to do, and sometimes she bumped into friends of Hereward's, people of his age, who looked at her with sympathetic curiosity, tried to think of something to say, and made her feel silly. There was a television near Hereward's bed, which perhaps she could have watched, but she could never make it work. It was not much of a life, all told, for Carina, now twenty-two, whose background had not equipped her to fend for herself in a foreign capital, nor to want to learn to do so.

When she heard the key in the door, there was no moment of pleasant anticipation that it might be the Padre, for it would always be Romola. Unless it was the cleaner, which was almost as bad; but at least Carina could foresee the cleaner's arrival.

'I'm afraid you must be missing Roger,' said Romola.

'I am,' said Carina. 'I am very sad.'

'Yes,' said Romola. 'What he told you must have been a shock for you.'

'Yes. But men are men.'

'I don't know about that,' said Romola, stoutly.

'It is because they are priests, not allowed to be married.'

'I don't know why that should make them go after children.'

'At home they do not, they have women. Can you say, mistresses?'

'You can indeed.'

Romola began to make a careful inventory of Hereward's pictures. 'Just to know what there is,' she said. 'We don't need to sell them yet, we have plenty of money from the rings. But no harm being prepared; and Rog can't do it now. Will you help me?' They did it together, moving from room to room. In Hereward's bedroom, which Romola had seldom visited, for even when Hereward was ill, he was always downstairs, she saw photographs of their parents, and one of herself. She did not let on to Carina that she noticed them. Now, of course, the room was very much Carina's bedroom, with the cosmetic whiff, and make-up on all the surfaces. But the duvet was pulled straight, the curtains were drawn back, and a window was open, all of which pleased Romola's critical eye.

'Would you like coffee?' Carina asked, when they had finished.

'No thank you. I'll go now.' Between a bad night following changing Hereward's manuscript, and the first full day of term, Romola was tired. 'I am sorry you haven't got the Padre coming over.'

'Yes, it is sad. But sad for you, very sad for you, with both your brothers . . .' Carina left her sentence unfinished, because she could not think of a term which covered the different plights of Hereward and Roger.

She did not need to, for Romola understood, and was touched to be thought of. Carina often surprised her. 'Thank you, dear,' she said.

Left alone, Carina sighed with relief and turned on the TV. She examined her nails, wishing the varnish was chipped or faded, but it was not.

Her mother telephoned, and they talked. Talking to her mother always made Carina want to be at home, and, now that she was without Roger, she was becoming more and more drawn to leaving London. It would be sad not to say goodbye to Hereward if he died, but he probably would not know whether she was there or not. Recently Carina had been having a bad thought, a thought she feared, and believed was a sin. It was that the longer Hereward lived, the less would be the money she would receive. If he lived on and on, she would get nothing. It seemed a waste, as Hereward was not happy and did not seem alive. Carina's mother had had a similar thought, and, when she had expressed it, Carina had been angry with her. It was the sort of thought you should never put into words. But Carina had it, herself.

~

Roger queued for the computer, hoping for something from Romola, but only found an email which dispirited him.

Dear Rog,

Well, here I am back in London. I am supposed to be being reinstated – but reinstated as a bishop? I rather doubt it. My wishes will be taken into account, I gather, and I think what I'd like best would be a parish. I enjoyed being a bishop, perhaps too much. Bishop at age 45 – I was not above dreams of being the second English pope! Not good for the soul. My time out has had me thinking. The landscape and the nuns did me good.

Rog, I hope there is something of the same for you. I know you are having a difficult time, and the grapevine has it that you are banged up at last. Three years is not too bad, I hope. Something off for good conduct. What will you do afterwards? Too early to think of that.

Tons of people to see and things to do. I plan to try to meet Gerry Farrell and his mother. Haven't worked out how to get in touch with them yet. I gather he tried to blame your abusee for inciting him to accuse me falsely, but the police weren't having it. So I'm not the only person Gerry slung mud at, fortunately in vain. He is a young man who needs a talking to, or a listening ear.

Love
Pip

To know Pip to be so cheerful, lively and good, to imagine him returning as a bouncing parish priest: this was difficult for Roger's dejected heart. He sighed, and wrote:

Dear Pip,

Well done. All well with you, and I am sorry you were ever accused. Indirectly, as I see from your email, Gerry's accusation of you is my fault, adding its extra kilos to so much that I have done wrong. Can't write more now, time on computer limited.
God bless,

Love,
Rog

Roger knew his email was self-pitying, but didn't have time to cleanse it of that. Now he would probably have to face a 'Poor old Rog, of course I didn't mean to make you feel guilty re Gerry!' type of email tomorrow. Easy to be generous if you are happy, if you are innocent, if you are respected, thought Roger. He left the computer to the next in the queue.

'Are we going to have that Mass?' asked Gandalf, waiting in the queue, as Roger passed. 'A few more people are getting interested in it, and some of the officers.'

~

Betty's cleaner did not think Betty should struggle up from the cellar with the chest of drawers, so she brought her husband over one evening. Together, with Betty gratefully hovering, they dismantled the little that had developed of Betty's studio and replaced the relegated furniture. Wisely, Betty did not tip the charming and burly Pole who had done all the heavy work, though she was sure

Jack would have, and would have got away with it. She thanked them and offered glasses of wine, but they had to get home.

Betty was glad to see Julia happy, and, thought Betty, Julia need never know of any maternal resistance towards the home-coming. No one need know. Julia was short-tempered, but Betty put that down to her condition. Some friends of Julia's, with whom, indeed, Julia was not short-tempered, came over with paint and ladders to redecorate Julia's bedroom and Mark's. It was time they were done, thought Betty. Betty could not look forward to the birth, but hoped she would fall head over heels for the baby when she saw it.

Julia was glad that Betty was becoming more reconciled to the change. For Julia, things were not simple. She thanked her stars not to have the additional task of keeping Betty cheerful and forward-looking. Betty seemed to be doing that for herself now. Julia was giving a paper at a conference in January, and had not yet been able to give it a thought. Occasionally, when work pressed, she wondered if she had done the right thing, but this question involved inspecting what life would have held if she had not taken the plunge, if she had not leapt before she looked. Then she felt reassured. In the spring, pregnancy would be over. That life-sized agenda-item – how to have a baby – had its box ticked. The biological clock was beaten. She was pleased and surprised that people were rallying round. Her position was interesting and, in her circle, unusual; and friends, whether couples or single, had their own curiosities, and their own various itches to be part of the story. They thought Julia was brave. They were not sure that she was as brave as they had supposed, when they saw what an excellent house she was moving in to, and that she had built-in childcare. But they were on her side.

~

Betty's telephone rang.

'Hello,' said Betty.

'Mrs Winterborne, you might not remember me. My name is Ayleen Brown, was Ayleen Ryan. I was at St Malachy's with Mark.'

'Oh, hello,' said Betty, all attention.

'My mother told me you had been asking if anyone remembered stuff about Mark. Is that right?'

'Yes, that's right. I've spoken to your mother and she has been very kind.'

'Yes. I've thought a lot about phoning you, and I don't know if it's a good idea or not. I mean, it's all so long ago, and nothing to be done about it now.'

'Yes?'

'Do you think there's any point. . . .'

'Ayleen, please tell me anything you remember.'

'Well, it's this. On the school trip, I was in the same tent as Mark.'

'Yes.'

'We only had one night there, the night before Mark – the night before the accident. In the middle of the night, Mark was crying. He was very upset.'

'What about?'

'I don't know. I thought he wanted you. I didn't know. He'd been perfectly all right at the bonfire. But when I woke up in the night hearing him crying, he was really upset.'

'What happened?'

'I went over to his sleeping bag and tried to cheer him up. I thought he was homesick. But he didn't speak, just cried. Then I went back to my sleeping bag, but I could still hear him crying, then I fell asleep.'

'Ayleen, thank you so much for telling me this.'

'I've got a boy of ten myself now, and I know I'd want to know everything, if it was him.'

'Yes. Thank you for telling me. Absolutely the right thing to do.'

'I hope you aren't too upset.'

'No,' lied Betty. 'Do you remember anything else, however tiny?'

'No.'

'What about the morning?'

'I don't know anything about the morning. I was helping with cooking; he was by the river.'

'He wasn't still upset?'

'Well I don't know. I wasn't with him.'

'I'll ring off now, Ayleen, but I'm very grateful.'

Betty put down the phone, and her composure collapsed. She put her head in her hands and cried. The idea of Mark missing her on the last night of his life broke her heart. If only she had known; if she had driven to the camp site, driven through the night; if her shape had appeared in the doorway of his tent; if she had pushed it open and picked her way in; if he had said, 'Mum?' Instead, she and Jack had been telling each other how pleased they were that Mark was keen on the school trip, and how good it would be for him to enjoy being away from home.

Homesickness is complicated. Betty began to wonder if anything had happened to set Mark's off. Could he have been bullied? Slight of stature and thoughtful of character, he might have been a butt for bullies, and his parents had rejoiced that he was not. For he was not. As explanations, they had thought of his sense of humour, his ready wit, and his friendly smile. They also noticed that he was someone the girls liked to take under their wings. Perhaps these things were protection enough, in a school which did not have a name for bullying. Or might Mark have hurt himself – burned himself, perhaps, at the bonfire, and said nothing about it? Or perhaps indeed said something about it, but to whom? Or – here was a thought – had Mrs Mace forgotten to hold him out, and had he wet himself?

By the time Betty went to bed, her heart in a vice of grief and pity, she had decided to email Father Roger Tree again, and take him up on the meeting he had offered. He had been on the trip. He might know something.

Chapter 14

Romola had to live with herself, as a person who was capable of changing someone else's manuscript. For an honest, earnest person like Romola, it was not easy. She would have found it difficult to explain to anyone else why she had done it; but then she would never have to. Sometimes, in the night, she thought she would email the publisher and retract her emendation. When morning came, she decided that what she had done was right. And so the days went past. She had an email of fulsome thanks from the publisher. As far as the publisher was concerned, her part in the matter was over. For all he knew she had not so much as read Hereward's manuscript.

She was glad that his terrible ending did not exist. She had annihilated it. Sometimes she thought that she had represented his hopeful side against his pessimism, as if she and Hereward were two in one flesh, or one in two fleshes. Then it seemed that in a complicated way she had done something morally right. Perhaps, in putting the book in her charge, he had issued a challenge to her, a covert instruction. Mostly, she knew that what she had done was morally wrong, probably, indeed, a crime; but, for her, inescapable. She knew, too, that something other than the desire for good to triumph over evil in the last extremity in the human heart had motivated her. It was her lifelong wish to be in charge of Hereward's fantasies. It was the same impulse as had led her to creep alone to the attic and stand up his disabled knight. There was defiance in it, and secret victory, victory which must never be detected. Further to this, was the fact that Hereward's novels were always published and hers never were. In this way, words of hers were going to be published in a novel. No one would ever know, but there they would be.

Sometimes she wondered what the reviews would say. Would it be more: 'The ending is poignant and of a tear-jerking beauty'; or, more: 'The ending betrays a loss of nerve, unusual for Tree at his best'.

She remembered to email the publisher the dedication to Carina that Hereward had wanted.

She had two dreams. Both of them took place in Hereward's house. In the first one, he was exactly as he had been in life. He was looking in the cupboard where his collections were kept, and was mildly surprised to find them gone. Romola said, 'We had to sell them.' He said, 'Ah, yes.' Then Romola said, 'I changed the end of your novel.' 'Ah, yes,' he said again. She must have intimated the nature of the change, for he said, 'Yes. A perfectly good ending. Just as good as mine,' and he turned and smiled at her. Then there was another dream, the same night, in which Hereward was trying to walk, but his body was ghostly and insubstantial, and his legs buckled mistily under him. Romola woke, sweating.

The day came when she deleted the original version of Hereward's novel from the recesses of her computer, keeping only the revised one. She reprinted the last page, so that the hard copy was exactly the same as the copy the publisher had received. She burnt the original final page. That was another landmark.

'You are so faithful,' said the nurse when Romola visited that afternoon. 'Is it a bit of a thankless task?'

'No,' said Romola.

'You come nearly every day. We know you are a headmistress. You must be very busy.'

'Head of department,' said Romola. 'Head of house. Not headmistress.'

'It must be burdensome, coming here every day.'

'He isn't a burden, he is my brother,' said Romola, misquoting a famous sentence which, from her face, the nurse did not know. 'Anyway, I would like to be here if he comes round.'

'If he came round we would telephone you soon enough, you may be sure.'

'I know you would. But one has one's dreams.'

She went into Hereward's room. Someone was sitting beside him. This was not an unusual experience for Romola. The friend sprang up to cede the chair to Romola. 'I'm just going,' he said.

'No change,' said Romola.

'No change. I'm so sorry.' They knew each other, but neither felt inclined to converse.

Romola sat. Hereward looked well. His colour was good, full as he was of nutrients, empty as he was of abusive substances. He was quite plump, now, for the first time in his life. What hair he had was fluffy and nicely combed. As Romola had observed before, the lines on his face were evened out. Except for the tubes, he looked as if he was asleep. He did not look quite like Hereward anymore; he looked like a waxwork of Hereward. Romola stroked his hand.

'Wake up, Hereward,' she said.

Carina came in. 'Were you speaking?' she whispered excitedly to Romola.

'Yes. But he wasn't.'

Carina was disappointed. She sat on the bed. This was not encouraged, because of all the delicate equipment both above and underneath the blanket. But they did it anyway, with great care.

There was a silence. Then, 'Have you heard from Roger?' Romola asked.

'Yes. A nice email. He says you queue to email, so it had to be short. It was not very short. He said what the food is like, not very nice, but he did not seem unhappy. They are sending him to another prison.'

'Yes. An open prison.'

'Not quite open? Or it would not be a prison.'

'A bit freer, I don't know how.' They lapsed into silence.

'Do you think Hereward will ever . . .?' Carina had asked this question so often that the sentence did not need to finish.

'We don't know.'

'I wonder about going home.'

'I'm sure you do, dear.'

'Do you think I should go?'

'I'm afraid I don't know how to advise you on that. If he came round, we would telephone you soon enough, you may be sure.'

'Soon enough?'

'I mean, at once.'

The three of them sat in silence. Normally Carina visited earlier in the day, not particularly wanting to coincide with Romola, although Romola no longer frightened her. Today Carina had come straight on from her class.

'Wednesday,' said Romola. 'You must have just had your class.'

'Yes,' said Carina. She had been wondering whether Romola was a lesbian. 'I would miss the people at my class, if I go home.'

Romola was silent. She was, as often, thinking about Hereward's absence. It was made more extraordinary by his presence. If he had been dead and buried, or dead and cremated, this long time, his absence would not have been a presence. And yet, how she clung to this absent presence.

~

Roger queued for the computer. Some people in the computer queue were chatty. Some were morose. He had got to know quite a few of his fellow-convicts by name. He himself was nicknamed 'Rev'.

He brought up his email and saw the name of Betty Winterborne. He turned white and his heart pounded.

Dear Father Roger Tree,

Thank you for your email. I am sorry I have not thanked you already. I would very much like to meet you, just to have a word about Mark on the school trip, if you would be so kind. I can fit in with you. You would be very welcome at my house, or you might prefer me to visit you. If the latter, let me have an address. Either way would suit me. I should like it to be as soon as possible.

Also, do you by any chance have contact details for Mrs Mace? I can't remember her first name. I have failed to get these through the school.

Yours,
Betty Winterborne

Roger stood up and fled the computer. 'That didn't take long, Rev,' said someone. 'What's the matter? Message from God?' But Roger had disappeared.

'Now comes my fit again, I'd else been perfect,' Roger said with Macbeth. What had just happened was worse than being in prison, more shocking, more horrible. And, unlike being in prison, it demanded a decision from him.

What should he do? The position was that he was about to be transferred to an open prison, probably in the next few days; so if he were to offer to see Betty Winterborne, she would have to visit him there. Did she know anything about his arrest and imprisonment? That had never been clear from her emails. For all he knew, she thought he was still a busy priest somewhere. Unlike the post, email does not give the game away.

Roger felt he had a duty to meet her. He would have to give her the address and visiting hours of the prison for which he was destined. He had already been issued with a wad of information about it, so this in itself would not be difficult. He sat down in his tiny room, and prayed. Tomorrow, when it came to his turn at the computer, he would have to tell her that he agreed to see her, that he was in prison, and that she could visit him. Any other course of action would be cowardice. But did the course of action which was not cowardice demand more courage than he had? He refused this thought. A thought that was not so easily rejected was that he could chat affectionately about Mark, and say nothing of what he and no one else knew. That picture had a strong attraction. It might indeed be the right thing to do, as any disclosure would devastate this woman, and, twenty-two years later, what could she do about it? Nothing. Unless she knew the nature of the crime for which he was behind bars, she would have no reason to suspect him of paedophilia, and therefore no reason to fear that he had interfered with Mark. He might, for all she knew, have been arrested for tampering with the church collection, or for GBH defending it. He had no obligation to be specific.

He could not plan, although his mind continued to do so, in myriad both devious and straightforward ways. He must wait and see how the conversation turned out. Perhaps the conversation would not happen. When she realised he was in prison, the idea of meeting him might go cold for her, or seem too momentous. It might indeed, if what she looked forward to was no more than a reminiscence or two from him about Mark on the trip. So much was unknown to him about Betty's state of mind.

The next day he sat at the computer and answered her email.

Dear Mrs Winterborne,

You may be surprised and shocked to learn that I am in prison. (Here he supplied the address and visiting hours.) *I should be happy to see you if you think the train trip worthwhile. Leave it a couple of weeks as I am being transferred. I know nothing of the present whereabouts of Mrs Mace, Marie, I think, though I'm not sure.* He then offered the easiest way in which she could advertise to the prison visiting service her intention and her chosen hour.

Yours,
Roger Tree

That was the best he could do. He was aware that his tone indicated an encounter that could be of no real significance. That tone had been impossible to avert. As it was, to press 'send' cost him more than he believed he had in him. He rushed away from the computer.

〜

152

It did not occur to Betty to be daunted by a prison visit. Roger was the only adult it was possible to be in touch with about the homesickness on the school trip. If she got no enlightenment from him, none of her speculations could be eliminated or re-inforced. Betty was sleuthing, and was ready to use any source that was to hand. The only source to hand, so far, was Roger Tree. She booked a visit.

She found she did not crave to tell Julia what was happening. What with sickness and moving house, Julia had her hands full. It came to Betty that she didn't want Julia's company on her prison visit. If Julia came, she would take over. Betty had not told Julia about Ayleen Brown's phone call. This was Betty's enterprise. It was the most adventurous thing she had ever done on her own.

Underneath Julia's immediate and more pressing preoccupa-tions lay a dull dread about her relationship with Betty. Julia had persuaded herself that what was happening was positive for Betty. It was not on Betty's behalf that she had qualms, but on her own. Betty would love the baby, and that would be that. They would be an elephant family. But they were not elephants, and Julia had begun to see the difficulties of her own role, the mother elephant, positioned between matriarch and calf. Betty had been a mother who knew how to keep a distance from a daughter. That precious distance was under heavy pressure now, and the pressure was set to grow heavier. Julia was afraid she had over-estimated her capacities not to be irritated by Betty. She had not overestimated them; she had simply not calculated them. Her heart had been fixed on having a baby before it was too late, and she could only see one way to do it, if her work was not to be a casualty. She had ignored the fine grain of the relationship between herself and Betty. Now that she was moving house, and now that she had so much to do with Betty, in terms of practi-calities, she was finding Betty annoying. Surprisingly, she had not foreseen this. She had not wanted to.

The obstetrician in charge of her case was a woman of about her own age. She had extracted from a reluctant Julia the tale of her circumstances, from how she had become pregnant to how she was planning to live with the baby. 'Well, I know I couldn't live full-time with my mother,' said she. 'Hats off to you.' But Julia knew it was not 'Hats off'.

And what if the calf became more attached to the matriarch than it was to the mother? Elephant mothers do not seem to mind this. But Julia might. She had not envisaged this risk until now. Would she regard it as a fair price to pay for the convenience of her circumstances? Or would it rankle?

Chapter 15

Carina was varnishing her nails at Hereward's bedside when she got the fright of her life. All the machines around Hereward began to flash like firework displays, and the most ear-splitting bells Carina had ever heard began to peal around her. She jumped up and ran madly to the window, varnish and brush leaping to the floor. She put her hands over her ears and emitted a series of sharp screams, which continued as the team rushed in and speedily stabilised Hereward. She was still screaming when they had finished their job. Her screams were rhythmic, panicky and loud, like an animal in a trap. A male nurse, still panting from his exertions, turned his attention to her.

'Are you all right?' he said, which was a silly question.

Carina could not stop screaming. He tried to pull her hands from her ears, and said, 'It's all all right now. We've sorted him out and he's fine. It's not the first time.' Then he added in a different voice, 'Please, please stop screaming. Sit down, please. I'll bring you a cup of tea.'

Now Carina was shaking, but managed to turn screams to gasps, and allowed herself to be led back to her chair. The nurse picked up the nail varnish and the brush. The brush had been trodden on, and was no good; but the lid of the bottle had broken from the brush and the nurse screwed it on. 'There,' he said. 'Not too bad, is it? You got a fright, that's all.'

'Did he nearly die?'

'Well, it was an emergency. Speed is the important thing.'

Carina had not met this particular nurse before, and liked him.

She liked the idea of men being nurses. She was charmed by his blue cotton two-piece uniform. 'What is your name?' she asked.

'Lennie. I know you, of course, we all know you. You are Carina, Hereward's fiancée.'

'Yes. I would go now, but I am meeting Romola here in half an hour. So I will sit here. But I am still frightened. Will the noise happen again?'

'Shouldn't. We've sorted him out. I'm going to bring you a cup of tea. You've deserved it.'

'Or will you stay with me, in case the noise . . .'

'Tell you what, while I get the tea, I'll turn off the bells. You saw the lights, didn't you?'

'Yes, they were terrible.'

'But not as bad as the bells?'

'No.' Carina shuddered.

'Keep an eye on the lights while I get the tea. I am putting this alarm bell in your hand, and if the flashing lights come on, press it.' Their hands touched, which was a pleasure for both. 'You see where to press it?'

'Yes, I see. Then you come at once?'

'Yes. It's very unlikely to happen. He hasn't had two cardiacs close together. So don't worry.' He smiled at her.

Her heart still pounding from shock, Carina sat with the alarm bell in her hand, a finger lightly laid against the point she might have to press. She sat still and upright, staring forward, like a good child. She looked at Hereward's face, as serene as ever. Hereward would not have wanted her to have to scream and scream. Tears prickled as she remembered how he protected her from anything nasty. Now he couldn't. She imagined him unbearably frustrated at not being able to look after her. Then she thought about the nice nurse, and the touch of their hands. She had been with Hereward since the age of nineteen, and he was her first love. There had been a boyfriend before, who had not meant very much, and she suspected of preferring his motor-bike to her. There was nothing in the world Hereward preferred to her. But some time, if Hereward did not get better, she would have to get another lover, or, better, a husband. At this prospect she felt shy, but interested.

She wished she could have left the hospital immediately, but she had arranged to meet Romola, for Romola was to give her particulars of how to visit Roger. Romola had already been to the prison, and knew what to do. So now Carina was waiting for Romola, and also waiting for her cup of tea.

Suddenly the lights began to flash. Carina looked at them. Her eyes were fixed on their now silent explosion of colour, mostly red. She looked at Hereward. He looked no different from usual. She looked back at the lights. Perhaps the lights were hypnotising her, she thought, or paralysing her. Her finger was touching the button on the bell the nurse had put in her hand, but she did not press it. She heard the words in her mind, 'Speed is the important thing.' But her finger did not move. She could see from Hereward's face that he was not in pain. If he were in pain, she would press the button at once; but his face registered nothing. Could he be dead? She waited. It was very strange to realise that she was in charge of the emergency team. She could call it, or not call it. It was more than a minute before she suddenly pressed the button. After she pressed it, she got up and stood against the wall, to be out of the way. Everyone rushed in again in their blue cotton uniforms, and crowded round Hereward's bed. Carina looked out of the window. She heard the team working. They were talking to each other, and using machines. She began to be aware that they were taking a longer time than they had earlier. She did not know what she wanted, or hoped.

After a while, there was quiet from the team, followed by whispers. Then a woman's voice said, 'Carina,' and Carina turned round.

Lennie and another nurse, not part of the emergency team, were looking at her. Their faces were sad and concerned. They said nothing for a moment, perhaps to let their silence prepare her for the news they must give her.

'We couldn't save him,' said Lennie.

'He has slipped away,' added the other nurse.

'But I pressed the bell,' said Carina.

'You did everything right. It's not anybody's fault,' said Lennie. 'It often happens when there's a second cardiac within minutes.'

Carina began to cry. Once she had started, she couldn't stop. She wailed, quietly. She was still quietly wailing, with both nurses at her side, when Romola walked in.

～

Sister Mandy Wall had intercepted Romola as she entered the building. She had been waiting. 'Romola,' she whispered, and Romola knew what she was going to say.

'He's dead,' said Romola.

'I'm afraid so.'

'My God.' Romola's bag slipped unregarded to the floor and she sat down heavily on a spindly little chair, more foyer knick-knack than piece of furniture. 'My God.'

Mandy Wall winced on behalf of the chair, despite the solemnity of the moment. Then she crouched down and took Romola's hand. But Romola did not like this, and stood up. 'I'll go and see him,' she said.

'I'll come with you,' said Mandy, 'and, of course, answer any questions you may have.' She shouldered Romola's bag.

To all appearances, Hereward was as always. Romola stood and looked at his face. The tubes had not been removed. There he was, as he had been for the past months. She touched his hand. It was as warm as ever. It came into her mind to ask how it was known so certainly that he was dead, but she did not, as that was a question a stupid person would ask. She sat down, as Carina did not seem to need the chair. Romola had taken in the presence of Carina, and the fact that two nurses were dancing attendance on her. So Carina had been here when he died. That was as it should be.

The waves and waves of the fact that Hereward was dead could not even begin to be assimilated by Romola, with four other people in the room and so much, presumably, that she would have to arrange. Her body felt different from hitherto, and the pressure of the chair on her back and buttocks was unfamiliar. It was a different world, now Hereward was dead.

'How did it happen?' she asked.

'He had two cardiac arrests within ten minutes of each other. He was stabilised after the first, but the second was too much for him. The team did everything they could.'

'I'm sure.'

'There was no pain.'

After quite a long silence, Mandy tried saying, 'You know, don't you, Romola, that the wonder is more that he lived than that he has died.'

'I suppose I know that,' Romola sighed.

Carina ran to Romola. She had stopped wailing when she saw Romola appear. Now there was an awkward hug. 'I'm glad you were here,' said Romola. 'What luck. You wouldn't have been here, at this time of day, if we hadn't been going to meet.'

'When you feel ready, if you would like to come to my office . . .' said Mandy.

'What about Carina?' said Romola.

'I want to go home.'

'You can't go home by yourself.'

But after a short deliberation it was generally deemed that she could, and that she would telephone her mother when she got in. A taxi would be called for her. So, still escorted by Lennie and the other nurse, Carina began to depart. Neither Romola nor Mandy found it easy to point out to her that she would not see Hereward again, but they both managed to mutter enough in the way of explanation to evoke a cry from Carina and to enable her to escape her bodyguards to the extent of stooping rather gingerly to kiss Hereward's forehead.

'We'll go to your office now,' said Romola. 'Then I'll come back here and say goodbye.'

'Of course you can always visit the funeral parlour, if you want to,' said Mandy.

After making the necessary arrangements, and learning that there would not be a post-mortem, Romola came back to

Hereward's room alone. The tubes had been removed, and his bed was tidy, as was his hair, which had anyway not been dishevelled for months. The hum and click of the machines was gone, and the room was very quiet. Only ordinary noises could be heard, the cooing of a pigeon on a nearby roof and, further away, London traffic going about its business. Hereward's hands were no longer folded together. Someone, perhaps a little foreign nurse from a Catholic country, had crossed his arms on his chest. Romola was touched. The new attitude imparted dignity and meaning to the fact that Hereward was dead, or so Romola found. Lying in his hospital bed, he had not looked awesome or admirable, until now. He had not looked as if he had learned anything from life. He was not more motionless, or not to the eye, than he had been before; but his appearance connected him to a quite different set of associations. Now he was a traditional dead person, whose battles had been bravely or adequately engaged with, and were over. He had exchanged the guise of care and life-support for the guise of effigies and brass rubbings. If anything were to be placed on his body now, it would be a sword, not a tube. To Romola he was the elder brother again, and what he had done today, because he had done it, she would be able to do, when her turn came. She touched his hand. It was still warm. His body had been warm for fifty-six years. How long would it take it to chill? Perhaps she should ask whether she could watch all night.

But the undertakers had been booked, and Romola did not want to be present when they took Hereward away. Their procedures might turn him back from fallen warrior into deceased hospital patient. Anyway, there was a lot to do, and only her to do it. So she found her bag, took a last look, and off she went.

When their father died, their mother did everything. Their role existed, but was secondary. When their mother died, twenty years later, Romola was the main organiser, but was helped by Hereward, and backed up by Roger. Now she was alone with it. When she arrived home she made a list, writing things down in the order they occurred to her:

- *Week's compassionate leave*
- *Register death*
- *Tell Rog*
- *Address book/phone calls*
- *Carina*
- *Notices Guardian and Times*
- *Funeral*

When she got as far as *Funeral* she halted. Burial or cremation? Her parents had a grave. It was not visited, but there they lay, together. Which would Hereward prefer? She would have to consult friends. She added to her list:

- *Consult re burial/cremation*

It was obvious that Hereward would not want church involvement, and Romola had a feeling a cremation would be simpler. However, friends might have views. Then she added:

- *Readings. What and who?*
- *Post-funeral do*

She missed Roger. He would have had a hot meal ready and would be someone to talk to. He would go round to Hereward's for the address book. Having had this thought, she went, herself. Carina was on the telephone. Romola was relieved not to have to talk to her. Romola waved, gesticulated an explanation, picked up the address book, and departed. Once home, she ate a bowl of cornflakes and poured herself a large gin.

She knew many of Hereward's friends, and began with the ones she knew. Breaking the news was a soothing occupation. Everyone minded so much. Everyone was sympathetic. A couple of the women burst into tears. Imparting what had happened helped Romola to know it was true. People wanted to talk about Hereward, and that was nice. Of course not everyone was in, and she had to decide whether to tell their machines, or phone again. She made a list, with ticks, noughts and question marks. She gleaned advice about arrangements, and decided to have a cremation. Then she rang some of her own friends. They also were comforting, and said they would come to the funeral. Everyone said that. Romola felt energetic, as if she was carrying out a task for Hereward, though she knew she was not. She had a couple more gins. A bit too late to be civilized, she rang her headmistress, and explained that she would be putting in for a week's compassionate leave. Her headmistress, also a friend, though not a close one, was grave and generous. The news would be all round the school tomorrow, thought Romola, with satisfaction.

She slept for a couple of hours; then got up into her dressing gown. She composed notices for the newspapers, only leaving blank the funeral arrangements. She sent an email to Roger. She hoped to have time to visit him before the funeral, so that he would not feel too left out. She didn't foresee his being terribly upset, though you never know. As soon as office hours began, she telephoned the crematorium which had been judged the most suitable by an advisor, and booked a time. A fortnight would elapse before the funeral, and she was pleased about that, as more people would be able to attend. She completed her notices to the papers and phoned them in. At some point she dressed, and went out to register the death. Everything she did revolved around Hereward, and this made her feel steady and excited.

She expected to feel flattened, later, with so much achieved, and less left to do; and dreaded that Hereward's death would hit her harder then. It was not quite like this, for the phone began to ring. It rang for several days. Some of the many phone calls involved volunteering for tasks – the post-funeral do was taken off her, including venue, food and drink. The funeral would be expensive. She kept doing sums about money, but making nonsense of them, because she persistently factored in what the nursing home cost weekly. By the same token, she could not take in that she did not need to find a daily time to visit Hereward. She set herself straight on these things again and again, to no lasting avail. She slept little and was never hungry. Carina and she went out for a meal together, neither with an appetite for it.

'I will go home now,' said Carina, pushing fish around her plate, 'home to Genoa.'

'Yes, of course,' Romola said.

'Mama and Papa are coming over for the funeral. I will go back with them.'

'That's a nice idea. I'm glad they are coming.' Romola gave up on the hamburger which she had chosen to give herself strength.

Obituaries. 'Survived by – whom?' asked the gentle voice on the telephone. Romola considered. Then she said, 'No one. Just don't have "Survived by".' Would she say a few words on Channel 4 news? No, she wouldn't. Was it true he had a novel about to come out? Yes, it was. There were many enquiries about the details of the funeral, from people who had not read the newspaper notice in full, but had picked up the telephone with a gasp on seeing Hereward's name. Complete strangers rang, having been given Romola's phone number by Carina when they tried Hereward's land line. Romola was patient.

Then there was the matter of the readings for the funeral. People said they would go away and think about it, but suggestions were few, and Romola could only think of the *Morte D'Arthur*. And who was going to read? Certainly not Romola. However, this began gradually to sort itself out. The strangest conversation for Romola was the following:

'I'm a friend of Hereward's and I do know you. Or, more accurately, we have met.'

'I remember your name, but can't put a face.'

'Never mind. I've seen the new novel, because they are trying to find a title for it, and they thought I might have ideas.'

'And did you?'

'Not yet. But I was just having a thought on a different matter.'

'Yes?'

'I'm wondering whether you've decided on readings for the funeral. If not, I have a suggestion. It's the last paragraph of the new novel. Shall I read it to you?'

'OK.'

He read the paragraph, at one moment his voice disrupted by tears.

'I don't think that's suitable,' said Romola.

'Why not?' The voice was piqued. 'Hereward was trapped, wasn't he, for the past months.'

'Yes, but he couldn't choose whether or not to free himself. And it's life that's freedom, in that paragraph, not death.'

'It was just a thought. I can bear to relinquish it.'

'If you come up with something else.'

'All right, I'll try. Plato? Dante?'

'Plato rather than Dante, probably.'

~

The second of the two weeks after the death, Romola had booked to go back to work, and take off only the Friday, the day of the funeral. At the end of the first week, she found time to visit Roger. It was her third visit to the prison, and, of course, her first since Hereward's death. She constantly noted things she was doing for the first since time since Hereward's death, and quite liked getting them over with. Walking round to his house; sitting down in a certain chair in her sitting room; going into a shop; washing her hair; even opening a tin of baked beans. Getting a train was quite a big one, in the huge but finite series.

Because of his bereavement, they gave Roger a room off the visiting room, a doorless cubicle, but relatively private.

'So it's happened,' said Roger. 'I'm so sorry. Not for me, not for Hereward. Sorry for you.'

'For goodness sake, Rog,' said Romola. 'I don't want to cry, here.' But she took her glasses off, and dabbed with her sleeve.

Roger was quiet and sympathetic, rather distinguished-looking in his prison uniform. 'I'm sorry I can't help you with anything. When Mum died, we were all there.'

'Yes. You did quite a lot of the address book.'

'Did I? Good.'

'Would they let you out for the funeral?'

'Even if they would, I wouldn't want to. Think of all the explaining and all the conversations I'd have to have. But I don't think they would, anyway.'

'Have you been upset?'

'To be honest, not really. For so long Hereward has been . . .' Roger gesticulated.

'Yes. But it isn't that, or not only that, because that's been the same for me, and, all the same, for me his death is an Exocet missile to the heart.'

'I'm sorry. But he didn't mean so much to me.'

'No. That's the real difference.'

'Yes.' Roger did not see fit to speak of his relief, to know that Hereward would never hear of his fall from grace.

'I don't think you knew him,' said Romola.

'Does anybody really know anybody?' asked Roger, and regretted it.

'Yes. Hereward and I knew each other. Insofar as knowing has any meaning.'

There was a silence, in which Roger felt told off for his priestly triteness. 'Would you say he had a happy life?' he asked.

'He knew ecstasy, he knew bliss. He knew contentment. He knew success, though that's of a lower order – at least, it is when you have it. He also knew anguish. He knew despair, in short bursts.'

'Terror?' Roger thought of Betty Winterborne, who was never far from his mind. Her visit had been displaced from its original date by the greater urgency of Carina's goodbye. But it was still approaching with alarming speed, and would happen two days after Hereward's funeral.

'No. Hereward would have been good in a war, except he would have doubted the justice of the cause.'

'You're making him sound perfect.' This had always been the way of it with Hereward and Romola, idealising each other. 'What about all those girls? He never settled down.'

'He loved each one of them. He loved Carina.'

'Why no children?'

'He had a vasectomy, you know.'

'Maybe, but why? That's not the real answer, any more than Hereward being out of it for so long is the real answer to why I don't care he's dead.'

'True. I know he didn't regret not having children.'

'Do you?'

'For me, do you mean?'

'Yes.'

'If so, it's so long ago. Yes, in a way. But how would it have fitted in to the rest of my life?'

'Do you think all three of us are screwed up about sex, in different ways?'

'You could see it like that,' said Romola, kindly hiding that she did not intend to see Hereward and Roger in the same bracket.

'Have you been to the funeral parlour?' asked Roger. 'We did with Mum and Dad.'

'We did. But no, and I shan't. But I have seen Hereward dead.'

Roger could not frame a question. 'How was he?' and 'Was he OK?' would not quite do.

Romola went on unprompted. 'He looked –' she chose her words carefully – 'very good.'

'Because, in the coma, he didn't look, I don't know, quite real.'

'No. That's hospitals. When he was dead, he looked wonderful.'

'I'm so glad,' said Roger. 'For you.' It was annoying to think of Hereward looking wonderful. Roger was sure he had just looked like an ordinary dead person, of which category Roger had plentiful experience. 'Who's reading what, at the funeral?' he asked, bracing himself to hear Hereward cracked up as a hero.

'It's been a puzzle. *Morte D'Arthur*, then there's some Plato. Shakespeare, Yeats, Hardy, all short-listed.'

'I've been re-reading *Howard's End* from the library here. I marked a bit for you, in case you think . . . I'm afraid it's rather short.' Roger found the place and read aloud: '"It is thus, if there is any rule, that we ought to die – neither as victim nor as fanatic but as the seafarer who can greet with an equal eye the deep that he is entering, and the shore that he must leave."'

Romola liked it. After a pause, she said, 'But it's not for Hereward.'

'Why not?'

'That's for an older person, who has thought about death. Hereward did not expect to die from his operation. He didn't prepare himself for death.'

'But I thought you said . . .'

'He had a worst case scenario, because he was a practical person. But that's different from being prepared for death. Which he wasn't. And he wouldn't have looked with an equal eye at the shore that he must leave, I can tell you, if it had Carina standing on it.'

'Carina would like a prayer.'

'Oh, golly, would she? I suppose she would.' This created a new worry for Romola. 'You must know everything about funeral prayers. If you think of an innocuous one, will you email it to me? Avoid the afterlife.'

Time was up. 'I really miss you, Rog,' said Romola, her mouth muffled in prison uniform. It was the most uninhibited hug these two had ever had.

'I'm sorry,' whispered Roger.

Chapter 16

Meanwhile, Carina was preparing to go home. She bought an extra suitcase for the clothes she had invested in during Hereward's illness. She went on a further shopping expedition and acquired a smart little black suit and new shoes for the funeral. She talked on the phone to her mother and other members of the family, but she was lonely. She was also anxious.

She was haunted by the minute that had gone by before she pressed the bell. It did not pass out of her mind, as most bad things always had. She did not know why she had waited, finger on the bell push. It was difficult for her to ask herself the questions that might have led to an answer. She flinched away from: Did I want Hereward to die? It did not remain a thought long enough to be tackled. It could not, because if the answer was yes, she would be a murderess. That was why the thought was always drowned out by a sound in her head like the rush and flapping of innumerable wings.

Carina was not used to the vagaries of the mind, let alone the complexities of guilt. They frightened her. She wanted them to go away, and they did not. She had no one to talk to. She did not confide in her mother. If anyone else were to express the thought that she was a murderess, she would feel even worse. So she kept the story to herself. No one else knew what had happened, and unless she spoke about it, no one could ever know. It was a secret. But the word 'secret' made Carina feel more, not less frightened.

When she had stolen her older sister's boyfriend, the bad feeling about it had worn off. When she had sex with the motor-cycle boy, the bad feeling had taken longer to wear off, but was gone as soon as she knew she was not pregnant. This bad feeling did not wear off. Carina had always slept well, but now she did not. She was afraid of a dream that might frame the question she must not ask.

One day she went to Mayton Road Nursing Home and waited to see the sister, Mandy Wall.

'What can I do for you, Carina?'

'I want to ask you something, Sister.'

'Go ahead.'

'Did Hereward have to die, when he had the second cardiac arrest? I mean, if the emergency team had arrived quicker, would he have lived?'

'Very likely not. Two cardiacs in a row are bad news.'

'But can you be sure that if the emergency team had been a minute earlier . . .' Carina was staring Mandy in the eyes with an intensely troubled expression.

Mandy took both Carina's hands. 'Listen, dear,' she said, 'it is quite natural that you should look for someone to blame, and that you should want to blame us. But I think it's safe to say we did everything possible. He had gold standard attention throughout his time here.'

'But if the team . . .' Carina was not finishing her sentences.

'You need to put this behind you and move on. Eventually you will. I know it's very hard at the moment.' Mandy was genuinely sympathetic, but did not want any trouble, let alone litigation. 'What are you going to do?'

'I am going home. My parents are coming for the funeral. I will go home with them.'

'Very sensible.' Mandy was relieved.

There was nothing more that Carina could say without arousing suspicion, and she left.

~

Mandy telephoned Romola.

'Carina's been here, and she's very worried.'

'Worried? Why?'

'I believe she thinks we didn't do enough to save Hereward's life.'

'Oh, nonsense.'

'I know. If she brings it up with you . . .'

'Yes, of course, I'll reassure her.'

'Thank you. One of us will be coming to the funeral. Probably me.'

'Oh, good.'

~

Carina's fears continued to gnaw and haunt her mind. She was not eating, and slept very little. Soon she did not even want to talk to her mother, because she was not telling her mother of what lay at the centre of her mind, avoided, but present. In a few days' time she was going to visit Roger, and say goodbye to him. She began to have the idea of going to confession to Roger. She knew that a priest is not allowed to say anything about what is said to him in confession. So her secret would be safe. And perhaps Roger would say she was not to blame. Roger might laugh at her fears. Then, if he laughed, her ordinary mind would come back to her, and she would move about the world as usual again. She would laugh at her own fears, on the train back to London. She would be convinced that, even if she had pressed the bell immediately, Hereward would still have died.

Sometimes the bad feeling seemed to be wearing off. She could forget about it. She had forgotten about it when she was choosing her suit for the funeral. She had forgotten about it during a session at the gym. But it came back. It came back more strongly, strengthened by its rest.

~

Romola's response to Mandy's phone call was to put Carina in charge of a finding a photograph, or photographs, for the funeral programme. This entailed Carina's being in Romola's house, for it was Romola who had always held the family albums. Romola

171

hoped that the combination of change of scene, a degree of company, and continued focus on Hereward would cheer Carina up. She was ready to pay the price of tripping on Carina and photographs all over her sitting room floor. Romola was impressed by Carina's choices. There was one of Hereward as a very young man, with a goat on his shoulder and a mountain behind him, laughing; and a recent one, gaunt and frail, but with a characteristic intent look. No one will start the funeral with a dry eye, thought Romola.

~

Carina arrived at the prison and went through the procedures that admitted her. It was good to see Roger. She clung to him and cried.

'Let's sit down,' said Roger. This was not a bereavement visit, so they were in the visitors' hall; but they had a table to themselves.

'You are in a uniform,' said Carina. 'Like a nurse.'

'How are you?' Roger asked.

'I am OK. I am sad that Hereward is dead.'

'Of course. You were there when he died.'

'Yes. It was peaceful.'

'I'm sure it was.'

'I have missed you, Padre.'

They chatted. Roger could tell that Carina was upset. Her appearance had not received its customary care. But this seemed normal to him, in the circumstances. He questioned her about her plans.

'So this is a real goodbye,' he said.

'Yes. It has been good to know you.'

'And you.'

'If you ever come to Genoa . . .'

'Yes, of course.'

There was a silence, while Carina's fingers played in her hair. 'Can I ask you something?'

'Of course.'

'Can I go to confession to you?'

'Why?' He asked this, although the answer was going to have to be no, as he no longer had the right to administer the sacraments.

'I am worried about something.'

Oh, dear, thought Roger, she has slept with someone. How entirely understandable. He had been surprised it had not happened before. Perhaps Hereward's death had liberated her.

'I'm sorry,' he said. 'I'm not entitled.'

Carina was disappointed. 'But you said words over Hereward to forgive his sins.'

'That was different. I did it because you wanted me to. Hereward was not a believer.'

'Nor am I.'

'Then why . . .?' Roger smiled at her, vainly inviting shared humour about her inconsistency. 'Look, the answer has to be no, very firmly. But, two things. One is, do be careful in future. The other is, why don't you go to Westminster Cathedral, if you want to go to confession? They have confessions all day.'

Soon it was goodbye, and the goodbye was smaller than it deserved. They had meant something to each other, but the goodbye happened at a moment when both were preoccupied with hidden knowledge, and they could not give themselves wholly to it.

Carina boarded the train for Victoria. She took a seat and looked out of the window. She did not want to go to Westminster Cathedral. She had no interest in that sort of confession, but wanted to tell the Padre what she had done, and that she did not know why, and have him laugh at the bad feeling until she too laughed.

Then she remembered Hereward. The family likeness between him and Roger brought him back to Carina in a sudden physical way, as the photographs had not done. She was aware of Hereward's smell. Present to her, as if he was beside her, were his warmth, his interest, his concern, his love. Suddenly she realised that he would not want her to be unhappy. Even if she had killed him, he would want her to be happy. He would much rather die than have her unhappy. He would chuckle over the idea that she was in a hurry to get her hands on what she stood to inherit. Everything turned upside down, and she felt that her bad feeling had been unkind to him. These thoughts rushed through her body in waves of conviction, joy and gratitude, and she began to cry. She wiped her eyes, and found that she was laughing.

~

Visiting over, the prisoners were in their cells. Roger picked up *Howard's End*, but found he did not want to read it. He thought of Carina, whom he would almost certainly not see again. He had never been closer to a woman than to her, except for his mother and Romola. What was this sudden sexual involvement in her life? Probably trivial. She was obviously not happy about it. He was glad her parents were coming to the funeral, and would take her home. They would look after her. It was time she had some ordinary family life. Once the probate was through, and Hereward's house sold, she would be a very rich woman. Would that be good for her? Might there be fortune hunters to cope with? She would have to manage as best she could. The mother seemed sensible. He felt curious about the father. Romola would describe him some day.

Thinking of Carina's father reminded Roger of the family photograph, and of Alessandro. He sighed.

He picked up his book again, but his mind was fidgeting its way back to Betty Winterborne. He could not prevent himself from rehearsing the dialogue. He knew this was pointless, because he could not foresee what she would say. And yet possible dialogues took place in his mind at all hours of day and night.

He reread a letter he had received that morning.

Dear Rog,

I was so sorry to hear about your brother's death. What a loss. And only fifty-six. But we can think of it as a happy release. Often that's a cliché but this time it isn't. I hope you are able to see it like that. Please accept my condolences. I see he has a new novel coming out, posthumously. I hope you feel he had a good life. From the obituary it seems at least to have been a full one.

I hope it isn't too bad where you are now.

There are rumours of a parish for me in the new year. It could be St Irenaeus, but this is confidential. I will let you know how things turn out.

Gerry Farrell and his mum both refused to meet with me. Oh, well.

With my best,

Love
Pip

Roger sighed again, bitter where he would have liked to be appreciative, envious where he would have liked to admire; and picked up his diary. He and a crooked accountant were starting a scheme for diary writing. Some interest had been shown, and exercise books for the purpose had been agreed and given out by the authorities. Roger and the crooked accountant had already assembled a group of six fellow-convicts, and numbers were growing, for the diary project caught on, and was becoming the fashion. The task was to write something, however brief, every day, and the diary group was to meet once a week, and read aloud as they cared to. At the end of a year, a book might come of it. So Roger kept a diary. Now he wrote:

I saw a wood pigeon out of my window this morning, in fact, two. Later, I saw a thrush, seagulls and two magpies. 'One for sorrow, two for joy'. So I am waiting, both to see more species of birds, and for the arrival of the promised joy. I am planning to ask if we can be allowed to feed the birds. It would take a bit of organisation, but not that much. A nice letter of condolence from my old friend Philip Jenkins. A nice chat with the chaplain, I highly recommend her company. An important day, for me. My brother's girlfriend, who is Italian, came to say goodbye. She is going home to Italy after my brother's funeral (tomorrow). So it was a sad goodbye. It is sad for me not to be able to be at his funeral. Emailed my sister to be of good heart tomorrow. Sausages, mash and peas for lunch, and a banana for pudding. Reading Howard's End *by E. M. Forster.*

Roger was struck by the amount of inauthenticity crowded into a short paragraph. What if he kept a truthful diary? It would have to say: *'Obsessive fear of Sunday, when I meet the mother of a child whom I abused and who died the next morning, a crime I have never confessed to.'*

Chapter 17

Romola dreaded Hereward's funeral. That is true, but it is also true that dread was only one of her emotions. She also felt strung up, and braced, as for a prepared and manageable ordeal. In the sleepless night that preceded that Friday morning, Romola ran through all her arrangements again and again. She knew who was going to be there early, bringing two hundred and fifty funeral programmes, with their two photographs of Hereward, which had come out well in the printing. She knew who was going to help give them out. The friend who had undertaken the music was reliable, and Romola had checked with her that all was well. The readers knew who they were, and were willing. The readings and eulogy had long since been finalised. Carina, Carina's parents, and Romola were to be in the front row. The pub for the reception was in walking distance of the crematorium, but for those who could not walk or had offered to be chauffeurs, there were enough cars to run that short distance. There were many things that Romola would not have thought of, herself, like how to secure parking in the precincts of the pub; but friends both of Hereward's and of her own had been competent not only to perceive but to solve a whole range of difficulties. The wheels were oiled before they started turning. Romola was reasonably satisfied with the old friend of Hereward's who was to give the tribute. The funeral programme directed everyone to the pub, and indicated that lunch, not just refreshments, was on offer. The friend who had undertaken the food, drink and venue was sure to have done a good job. It was lavish, and Hereward's estate was paying. In the teeth of all this, Romola was afraid that something would go wrong, that there would be something unprepared and unforeseen, to which she would have no solution.

Sometimes she thought that what was going to turn out to be unprepared, unforeseen and insoluble was simply how devastated she was. But that must wait until after the funeral. Hereward's 'good send-off' was what mattered, until it was safely over. Romola had been at full stretch since Hereward died. She had taken five days compassionate leave, but the following Monday, now last Monday, she was in school as usual, to work a four-day week. Entering the school gates, and the staffroom, and the classrooms, were very big post-Hereward first times for Romola, and she was glad to get them behind her. Sometimes she felt as if organising this funeral was the only thing she had ever done in her life without Hereward; but she reminded herself that this was not actually so, for he had no part in the challenges and successes of her work life. But that remained the feeling. It was part of missing him.

Friday was overcast, but dry and not cold. Romola was so early at the crematorium that the funeral before Hereward's was only starting. She parked in a remote bay and wished she still smoked. Her clothes had been a worry – her dark suit was a bit tight since Roger's good meals, but she decided to wear it anyway, with the waistband inconspicuously undone. She looked at herself in the car mirror, and combed her hair. Her face was tired and strained, but everyone would forgive that. People would be kind to her, and she must not let that make her cry. And she must be careful about her drinking. These resolutions taken, she watched the people emerge from the crematorium, gather together, then disperse. She hoped the flowers belonging to that funeral would disappear before her hearse arrived, with its huge influx of wreaths. Someone had arranged for Hereward's flowers to be collected later for an old people's home. Romola herself had not supplied flowers; not able to contemplate what to write on the label, and guessing, furthermore, that the flowers were doomed, sooner or later, to become a nuisance to somebody. Where Hereward's ashes would be scattered was not a question for now. As to collecting them, she had ascertained that she would be able to do it tomorrow. This thought turned her heart over.

Ridiculously early, she got out of her car and went to the crematorium entrance. She hung about, firming up the unfastened waistband of her skirt, and unbuttoning then rebuttoning her jacket. Before she had time to worry about it being late, Hereward's hearse arrived, and she made contact with the friendly, solemn undertakers, the chief of whom she had already met. She saw a car in the distance, and recognised it as belonging to the friend with the programmes. So far, so good.

People began to arrive. All came up to Romola for a word or a hug, took their programmes, and found places in the benches of the crematorium. Romola remained outside, greeting. She greeted her friends, friends of Hereward's, mutual friends, professional acquaintances of his, and sometimes, the famous. Her worry at this point was whether everyone would be able to fit into the crematorium, and, indeed, by the time she turned and went in, it was very crowded, with standing room only at the back. Mandy Wall had to stand. Carina and her parents arrived, Carina ravishing in her closely fitted black suit, her radiance and lustre restored. Romola, the last to enter, joined them in the front row.

'I have no hat,' whispered Carina. 'Many of the ladies have hats. Mama said I should have a hat, but I didn't think so. Now I think she was right.'

'Never mind, you look lovely,' said Romola. 'I am not wearing a hat.' She knew this would be cold comfort, for it was not with Romola that Carina was likely to compare herself.

The ceremony began. A friend had tipped Romola off to book a double session, but, even so, it seemed to pass quickly. The tribute was mumbled, and must have been inaudible to those at the back; but, generous or narcissistic, the speaker had brought printed copies that could be distributed. When the moment came for the coffin to disappear into the fiery furnace, Romola looked away.

The next worry was whether everyone was going to fit into the room above the pub, but when the time came, the nice official kindly opened an adjoining room, which they could also use; and all was well. So far, so good, and, now, much further. Further still, when it became clear that the drink was plentiful, the food good, and that there were a number of young people with trays to distribute both. It was finger-food, but the portions were sizeable and the variety endless, and enough of them readily added up to a lunch.

Romola thought that everybody wanted to talk to her, and no one wanted to talk to her. Everyone wanted her to know they had been thinking of her, as well as of Hereward, in these past months, and some wanted details of his decline. They tended to cap his death with deaths known to them. Others enquired solicitously how she was coping. Romola was polite, but did not warm to these topics. She would have liked to talk about Hereward. Only a few people knew how to do this to her satisfaction, and realised this was what she would like. Several of these looked at the photos on the programme with her, and cried, and reminisced, and this suited Romola perfectly. People drifted away from her very easily, into knots where less intractable subjects than death could be canvassed. The gathering quickly became a party. Encounters happened, some after years, a few, thrilling. Gossip, views, books, illnesses, politics and current affairs were soon what were filling the air.

Carina and her parents knew no one, of course, and, before the end, Romola found she preferred to be with them. She had a useful conversation with Carina's father, a handsome and burly businessman, with tidy grey hair and a lovely smile.

'We know Hereward has left everything to Carina,' he said. 'Is that all right for you?' He asked the question tentatively, kindly. Romola could see he was a good man.

'Yes,' she said. 'Anyway, I've got the literary stuff.'

He was relieved. 'Ah, yes,' he said. 'A great writer. I have seen a film which Carina says is from a book, a book he has written.'

There was a brief silence, before he returned to his topic. 'You must choose what you want, furniture, pictures. Then I can see to the sale of everything, and the house, in time, later.'

'Will you come over, to do that?'

He laughed delightedly. 'It can be done on the internet,' he said.

'What, auctions of pictures, a house, everything? On the internet, from Genoa?'

He mimicked the smile of a magician, but it did not make him unattractive. 'Everything,' he said. 'If I have to come over, I come over.' Then he said, 'I liked Hereward.'

'I'm glad,' said Romola. 'But you must have felt he was much too old for Carina.'

'Of course. More than thirty years.'

'Age difference. Too much.'

'Too much. I am two years older than Silvia. That is better.'

'Thirty years better.'

'Also he was not a Catholic.'

'No. I hope you noticed there was a prayer at the funeral.' Roger had come up with Cardinal Newman's famous prayer, 'May the Lord protect you all the days of your life', with its tear-jerking ending, 'peace at last', and Romola had found a good reader for it, and had put it at the end.

'My English is not good enough,' he said.

'Your English is excellent,' answered Romola, and the conversation deteriorated. He had his eye on his watch, anyway, for there was a plane to catch. 'Carina will leave her key in the house,' he said. He was evidently a man who thought of everything.

'She can keep it,' said Romola. 'It's her house.' But his good manners would not permit this.

The glamorous and behatted Silvia was not part of this conversation, for she had found someone to talk to about cottages in northern Italy. Carina had fallen in with the caterers, who were the only people of her age, and was causing a stir amongst them.

Romola overheard an exchange. 'You know he left everything to that girl.'

'Which girl?'

'What do you mean, which girl? Look over there.'

A few seconds' silence. 'Well, I'm not surprised!' A brief, unspoken moment of marital discord. It was his tone of voice.

So the terms of the will had got around. Romola did not want people to think she had been cut out, or had done badly, or was hurt, or being noble. Hereward's stuff and the house would have been nothing but a bother to her, and she had no wish to be rich. She would have an inheritance, in any event, probably a princely one, from his literary estate. But from this moment of the proceedings, she began to see people's compassionate glances in a new light, and did not like it, and wished the occasion would end. It occurred to her that more wine might help her get through what remained of it, but she wisely resisted.

She shook hands cordially with Carina's parents as they began to collect their daughter and bustle off, but did not expect what happened next. Carina threw her arms round her, weeping. It was a long hug. Carina said, 'I will never forget you, Romola, you have been so kind to me.' Romola wished that were more true. She held Carina carefully, warmly, unreservedly, for she had in her arms what was, to Hereward, the pearl of great price, the eighth and greatest wonder of the world. This was the moment of the day when Romola came closest to breaking her resolution not to cry. She clenched her face against the tears, and hugged Carina, and gently stroked her shoulders. She could not speak.

Soon goodbyes became general. Two of Romola's friends were to come home with her.

'At the crematorium we can retrieve the labels of the flowers – the messages,' said one of them.

'The undertakers do that,' said Romola. 'They'll send them to me. It's part of the service.'

The friends, who were lucky enough not to have been closely involved with undertakers as yet, were impressed. The three women walked back to the crematorium and Romola's car. Romola drove to her house. She appreciated her friends' not wanting her to be alone. But she was too tired to enjoy their company for long. She did not agree when they suggested opening a bottle of wine. They saw how she felt, and left her to herself.

Evening was coming on. Romola changed into comfortable clothes. She stood and looked out of the window of her bedroom. So this was the world without Hereward. She wondered what was left of her, and, for the first time for weeks, thought of Mrs Gaskell and *Wives and Daughters*. She knew immediately that this was a project she would not touch again. Perhaps a certain verve and inventiveness which came out in her when she wrote was gone for ever. Over time she would take stock of what was still within her. She did not know, yet. She felt like someone whose body has been badly smashed, and who finds out, gradually, over months, which powers recuperate, and which never do, which regions have been hard hit, and which have escaped.

But this was to think about herself. What of Hereward? What had it been like for him, whom she knew so well, and who, recently, had become such a mystery? He had certainly not expected to die, at the time when he went under the knife, though he had made provision for it. Still less had he expected a coma. Had Mr Bleaney mentioned the word coma, hurrying through the ward with the consent form? She would never know. If so, it would have been a new thought for Hereward. Did it raise a qualm, or did he ignore it? If only, if only . . . If only the word 'coma' had made Hereward say to Mr Bleaney, 'Sorry, after what you've told me, I'm going home,' and then begin to struggle into his clothes, pant, sit on the edge of the bed, take a pill, phone Carina, and pick up his stick. If only, if only. What had it been like for Hereward, to be in a coma? With his brain half gone, perhaps like nothingness. Had death been any different to his previous state, for him? Probably not. And yet Romola did not approve of agreeing that Hereward had died, effectively, at the start of the coma. He had still been there, warm, living, enigmatic. Did she wish they had let him die, during the operation, instead of dragging him back? In a way, yes; but no. She had continued to know and love him, and so had other people, sitting quietly by his unresponsive body. But had that been unfair on him? He would certainly not have wanted Carina to see him like that, devoid of manliness. But he had no choice.

The telephone rang and it was Roger. 'How are you doing?' he said. 'I thought you would be home by now.'

'Yes, I am.'

'And how are you?'

Romola did not answer at once, then said, 'I think I'm putting a toe in the water of what it is like now.'

'Yes, poor you. Was it a good send-off?'

'It was. Everyone came. Everything worked as it should.'

'What was Carina's father like?'

But Romola could not chat. 'I'll come and see you soon, Rog,' she said. 'Talking to you has put another quarter toe in the water.'

Other people telephoned, some to commiserate afresh, some to congratulate her on the funeral, some to do both. Romola did not want long conversations. She did not know it yet, but she was very tired. Before she went to bed, Carina telephoned from Genoa.

'Are you all right, Romola?' she said. 'I am crying to think of you.'

'You are an absolute darling to ring me,' said Romola. 'I can see why Hereward loved you so much.'

~

Romola slept better than she had of late. She woke calm, slowly remembered, and remained calm. She felt as if she had dreamt of Hereward, though the dream itself she did not recall. She lay quietly in bed, revelling in the fact that he felt near. Then she got up and looked out of her bedroom window. This was the morning view of the world without Hereward. It was better. She was not going to see him again, and she would always have to do without him. But she was not afraid. She felt one with the countless numbers of other men and women who face their future without their mainstay. It can be done. She would do it.

In a spirit of soldierly self-care, worthy of the vast army into which she had been enlisted, she made herself eggs on toast for breakfast, and ate every morsel. Then she spoke on the telephone to the two friends whose ministrations she had failed to respond to after the funeral. Then, in a moment of weakness, she rang Hereward's landline. Five rings. 'Hereward Tree. Sorry to be unavailable. The beep is coming now.' Beep. Silence. Romola put the phone down. She rang it again. Then a third time, to catch the intake of breath before: 'The beep'. How could he be dead?

Then she pulled herself together and stacked up the essays she had to mark before Monday. But she could not look at them. She stared out of the window at the leafless trees, a squirrel, and a couple of pigeons. All she seemed to be good for was sitting and staring; but she knew this would pass. She made herself a cup of coffee, and prepared to go to the crematorium to collect the ashes.

A funeral was about to start when she arrived – flowers, hearse, dark smart clothes, so reminiscent of yesterday – but she found her way to something like an office. She had brought her passport, in case there was security around the retrieval of ashes. But she and the woman on duty recognised each other, so there was no need for identification. The woman handed Romola a taped up cardboard box, heavy, but perfectly possible to carry. Her manner was a mixture of the cheerful, the matter of fact, and the reverential, and Romola thought years of experience had gone into that combination. Romola went straight back to her car, and placed the box on the passenger seat.

Now she wished there had been a burial, instead of a cremation. She had yielded too readily. And when she gave the go-ahead to cremation, she had certainly not foreseen this moment. If there were a grave, with Hereward newly in it, she could think of his body lying as it was in death. And she would be able to choose a tombstone inscription. The process of decomposition would be slow, and, if she was lucky, keep time with her capacity to relinquish. This was too quick. And the box was too small to represent a person, and made of cardboard. Somehow she had expected an urn, or some other receptacle of greater gravitas. But it could not be helped. She drove home.

She put the box on a low table in her sitting room, and sat down near it. Another problem about the ashes was that they were open to ridicule, evoking jokes such as: 'We must get around to scattering Auntie Amy, she's still on the mantelpiece'. Romola thought that the sooner she got these ashes scattered, the better. But she did not know where to scatter. Hereward was not a place person. And she could hardly inflict them on Carina, which is where they belonged emotionally. Hampstead Heath, where he walked until he became too ill, walked reluctantly and under doctor's orders, might be as good as anywhere. But perhaps that was not allowed. She could consult people. There were people she could consult. There was her own small garden, of course, of which Hereward had never taken the least notice; but that would mean she could never move house, to downsize, in retirement, if she wanted to. Or could she? It was impossible to know in advance what forms relinquishment took. His pretty but neglected garden, with its apple tree, would not do, of course, for that house would be on the market in no time.

Romola fetched some scissors, and addressed the tape that bound the cardboard box. The lid came up. Inside the box was a bag of clear polythene, through which the ashes could be seen. She pulled the top of the bag apart, and put her fingers into the ashes. They were not fine, but grainy. Romola was surprised. She had expected them to be light and delicate, like the ash of a wood fire, or a cigarette. She would have preferred that. It must be the bones, she thought.

She sat and stared. There was no happy ending she could impose on this story. It was intractable to the magic potion with which her characters were liable to rush to the rescue in Hanulaland. The final paragraph as he had written it, now lost forever, had, perhaps, the last laugh. And yet that is not how Romola felt. She was aware of the beginnings of a sense of steady strength, which took death into account without being overwhelmed by it. We all have to die, she thought, and, whether by earth or fire, or indeed by air or water, our bodies will become a handful of dust. As with blowing her nose, tying her shoelaces, striking matches, doing long division, Hereward had shown her the way. But why did he have to go so early? If Romola did a Mum, she would have forty years without him. She quailed; then rallied. She must hang on to the new strong feeling, so as to be ready for anything.

Chapter 18

Julia no longer felt sick. Indeed she felt very well. She was still taking care not to lift things off high shelves, for fear of miscarrying. The antenatal clinic was pleased with her progress, and she did not have to see much of the obstetrician she had found a challenge. The house move was also going smoothly. There were several offers on her flat.

One evening Tony finished the job. He cleared up. Julia did not tell him she would be deserting the flat without having had more than a taste of his cupboards, his shelves, his airing closet. She did not want him to know that as far as she was concerned his work was wasted; and she did not tell him that she was moving in with her mother, or that she was pregnant. Tony knew the career Julia, Dr Winterborne; and Julia did not want to blur the clear and tidy edges of that person.

'You've helped me,' Tony said as he packed up.

'Ah yes, the nevus.'

'The what? Oh, yes. Not only that. Talking to you. About Father Rog. About my parents. Baz.'

'Well, it's been a pleasure.'

Tony solemnly handed her the key, as if it were a rite. 'Call me if there's anything else I can do here,' he said.

She went to the front door with him. 'I will. And I'll recommend you.'

Early in the carpentry project, she had taken pleasure in transferring her possessions from their removal boxes to the cupboards and shelves, as these appeared. Now it didn't seem worth it. For one thing, she should not lift anything heavy; for another, they might as well stay in their boxes, now, and be thus transported again to their more permanent destination. So it was that some of Tony's storage, beautifully sanded and smelling of wood, lightly and transparently varnished, was to remain pristine until Julia's successor moved in.

~

'Horrid having to leave my flat,' Julia said to Betty.

'Horrid? I thought you were longing to.'

'Longing to? No, not longing to. I have to.'

'You've so thrown yourself into all the changes here, I thought you were happy about it.'

'I have to do it, because of the baby. But of course it's a wrench to have to give up my own space.'

'Poor darling,' said Betty.

After a silence, Julia said, 'I'm having the ultrasound tomorrow.'

'I don't think we had that in my day.'

'You must have.'

'Perhaps we did. Do you want me to come with you?'

'No, of course not!'

'Sorry.'

'Look, I'm nearly forty, the scan will be in my own hospital, I know everybody, why ever would I want my mother to come with me? Do you want me to seem a complete freak?'

~

It was Sunday. Betty sat on the train, having checked its Sunday time, and wondered whether to make a list of topics. What, exactly, did she want to ask Roger? She knew from Ayleen Brown that Mark had been upset during his last night. Did Roger know anything about what had caused the upset? Betty would have liked to ask this question of Mrs Mace and the other two teachers on the trip, but they had melted away. Roger, brought to light after years by the paragraph in the local paper, was the only adult participant in the school trip whom she could trace. That was his importance, and the reason for the visit.

Probably Roger Tree would have nothing to say. What would he have known, and what, had he known anything, would he remember? Trivial distress from homesickness or a tiff with a best friend was hardly the sort of thing that would stick in a busy man's mind for twenty-two years, even if Roger had got wind of anything at the time. If Mark's eleven o'clock routine had been forgotten, and he had wet the bed, he would have been distressed; but no one would have known. Roger Tree would probably listen to her questions, and be sympathetic, in a priestly sort of way, and then she would get the train home. But still, it was worth doing.

So Betty looked out of the window of the train. It was beginning to be a wintry landscape. A few leaves still clung to some of the trees. For the first time since early spring, Betty was wearing her warm coat. She enjoyed train journeys, as long as she knew where to get out, and what to do then, and had enough money on her for the unexpected. She had never visited a prison before, and hoped she would cope dauntlessly with whatever the routines were for getting in, and arriving at the right place. She had brought her passport, in case. She had also brought a book, but she did not read. Her thoughts rambled through her head, and she looked at the cows. She was due at the prison at three o'clock, and four o'clock was closing time.

So, at last, Roger and Betty met. They met one on each side of a table in a long hall. There were a number of other tables, at which other prisoners were entertaining their visitors. The tables were sufficiently far apart for private conversation. Children ran in the aisles, but they were not meant to, and were rebuked by officers. But what else could they do, while their parents talked? Betty smiled at one of them.

Roger Tree looked quite different from how Betty remembered him. He had been handsome, with thick fair hair, and a pleasing look of well-being. Now the fair hair was very thin, and his face was haggard. He was still handsome, if good features are enough; but Betty thought he looked terrible, and that his appearance showed the ordeals he had been through. She sat down, feeling sorry for him. Roger was paler and more drawn even than usual, because of his terror of this meeting. He saw in front of him an elegant woman he would not have recognised, with plenty of greying hair pinned up on her head, giving her, to Roger, an old-fashioned air. He had visited Mark's family once or twice after Mark's death, bluffing it out, persona grata because he had risked his life. He remembered Jack no more vividly than he remembered Betty, though he did remember being afraid of Jack.

'I just wanted a chat with you,' said Betty, 'about Mark and the school trip. If you can cast your mind back.'

'Yes, I'll try,' said Roger.

'It's this,' said Betty. 'Do you remember Ayleen Ryan?'

'No. Was she a teacher?'

'No. She was a little girl in Mark's form.'

'OK. I don't remember her, but . . .'

'That doesn't matter.'

Roger was taken aback by the tone of Betty's voice. Contrary to appearances, she was someone who could take charge.

'That doesn't matter,' Betty said again. 'She is now an adult and a mother. Recently it occurred to her to tell me something that happened on the night at the camp.'

'Strange,' said Roger, his mouth dry. Could she have seen anything? He cleared his throat and swallowed. 'Strange, to tell you something now, so long afterwards.'

'Yes.' Betty did not go into how and why she had resurrected her acquaintance with Ayleen's mother. 'Ayleen told me that she woke up to hear Mark crying in their tent, and she crawled over to him, and he was very upset.'

Roger was silent, attentive. It did not sound as if Ayleen had seen anything.

'She suggested to him that he wanted his mother, me. This made Mark cry more, and Ayleen thought she had got it right. But then she was too cold and went back to bed. That's all. But since I knew this, I have been wanting to see you. You are the only adult from the trip I have been able to track down.'

Tracked down, perhaps, wondered Roger, by dint of his name's small and infamous appearance in the press?

Betty went on, feeling she had not made herself clear. 'What I am asking, is whether you can think of anything that happened that might have upset Mark that night. Anything at all.'

Roger had two feelings. One was fear. How would this woman cope with knowing what he could tell her? And if he did tell her, she would be entitled to go to the police, and his sentence would be lengthened. Worse, much worse, his disgrace would be more than doubled. Trebled, because of his long reticence. He had become used to living with the amount of obloquy Tony Tremlow afforded him, and no one in Church or State suspected more. This story – a ten-year-old, a death – would be much worse.

The other feeling was that he should tell Mrs Winterborne the truth. This was not an unexpected feeling, and it was because of it that he had so dreaded this meeting. He had never seriously thought he would lie. He knew she deserved to know. It was a matter of justice. What he had not expected was that he would want to tell her. He had a crazy idea, looking into her kind, anxious face, that she might forgive him.

Roger realised that what he said now would be decisive. If he started the story, he would have to go on with it. He took a deep breath, and leaned forward. 'I do know,' he said.

'Tell me.'

'The children were in their tents, asleep. Mrs Mace and I, and two other teachers, were round the camp fire.' Roger did not say, 'We were drinking,' for fear that Betty would think he was advancing an excuse. 'Mrs Mace said she hadn't held up Mark to pee yet, and she should have, and would I do it.'

'Yes?'

'I got him out of his tent and walked him to the hedge. He was half asleep.'

Betty nodded. She knew exactly how he would have been.

'He peed.'

'Go on.'

'This is the difficult bit. I asked him to touch my penis.'

'And?'

'And he did. Then I took him back to his bed.' Roger found it impossible to say that he had ejaculated all over Mark's pyjamas. He hoped he was saying enough, without that.

'You asked him to touch your penis. And he did, of course.'

'Yes.'

'Poor darling.' There was utter silence between them, with distant noises of other colloquies and of running children.

'I should say more,' said Roger. 'I was in love with Mark. I liked to watch him, I sought occasion to go into his form room, I had little conversations with him at odd moments. He was very lovely. I knew I loved him. I didn't think it was sexual. No, I knew it was sexual, but . . . Well, I didn't think anything would ever happen. Without the school trip, it wouldn't have.'

'That's no excuse.'

'I know. It's not meant to be.'

Anger was not Betty's strongest feeling. All her faculties were levelled at trying to imagine the situation for Mark. She had speculated constantly since Ayleen Brown's phone call, without enough information. Now she imagined the situation afresh, rapidly factoring in these harsh and horrible pieces of reality. Mark had gone to sleep in his tent, contented, coping with the school trip, among friends. Being held to pee, he would scarcely have woken. That was his way. Then he would have come to, to hear Roger telling him to touch his penis. He was not a child who disobeyed grown ups. He touched Roger's penis. She could have hoped that he was too sleepy to notice, and that he went straight back to sleep with the first touch of his pillow, and by morning thought it was a dream; but she could not imagine it like this, because of the upset.

'Didn't you know he was upset?' was her first question.

'No.'

'You bloody fool.' Betty had never spoken to anyone like this before. Her tongue was loosened.

Shocked, Roger said nothing.

'Did you have an erection?'

'Yes.'

'You little shit.'

'I know.'

Betty was silent, looking at the table, imagining. 'Did you say penis, or willy?'

'Willy.'

Silence again. Then Betty said, 'Anything you haven't told me? Tell me everything.'

'Not really.'

'Did you come?'

Silence from Roger. Then, 'Yes.'

'Call yourself a priest. Call yourself a human being.'

'I know.'

Now Betty's tears began to flow. She thought of Mark, upset in the tent, wanting her. She thought of how bewildered he must have been by Roger's request. She thought of Mark standing by the hedge, droopy with sleep, or perhaps already upset, having to wait for this monster to come.

'Did it take you long to ejaculate? How long did he have to stand in the cold?'

'Seconds.'

Betty hoped this was true. She was silent, the sequence of events branding itself into her consciousness. 'Did you touch him?'

'Only the amount I had to to help him pee.'

Betty was silent again, concentrating, taking everything in, building her story.

'Are you glad you know this?' Roger ventured. He did not like the sight of all these tears.

'Yes.'

Fury was beginning to gain the upper hand, for Betty. 'Do the police?'

'Do the police what?'

'Know this.'

'No.'

'I could inform them.'

'Yes.'

Hearing this 'Yes', it crossed Betty's mind that it had been brave of Roger to talk to her as he had. He had known the risks, and gone ahead anyway. She gave him no quarter for this.

'I'll have to decide what to do about that.'

'Yes.'

'If Jack was alive, he would kill you.'

Roger said nothing.

'What about the next morning?'

'The next morning.'

'Yes. Tell me in detail. When did you first see Mark?'

'I watched him come out of his tent. With the others.' Roger did not like to say that between lust satisfied, and terror of discovery, he had no longer been watching Mark with the eye of love, but with an ignoring eye.

'Did he look around, looking for you?'

'I don't think so,' said Roger, who would not have known. 'He seemed OK, with the others,' he added lamely.

'Then what?'

'Then we got involved with cooking breakfast. I felt terrible of course.'

'Don't bother me with that.'

'OK. Some of the children were helping with breakfast; some were playing. Then we were alerted to a group by the river. You know the rest. It was all in the inquiry.'

'No. It wasn't. What happened when Mark was standing on the stone, and he saw you?'

'Nothing. I was worried – we were all were – and I went in.'

'Did he know it was you who went in to save him?'

'Yes.'

'Good.'

Betty was silent. She was still crying, and, her tissue soaked, was using a pretty Italian silk scarf that had been round her neck to mop up her tears. She was continuing to imagine. Then she said, 'We have to think about how much his death was connected to the night before – to what you'd done.'

'Yes,' said Roger. He added, 'We can't know.'

'That's why we need to guess. Mark had been very upset in the night. We don't know when he got to sleep, because Ayleen's account ends. But he tumbled out of the tent in the morning with the others, looking, as you report, fairly normal. Then he became one of a group that went to the river bank, and the only one of that group to jump on to the flat stone. Why did he do something so dangerous?'

'There might be no connection between that and what I did. I have thought about this a lot.'

This last sentence annoyed Betty. 'I don't think we can take your thoughts very seriously. Of course you want to disconnect the two events. But I don't think so. I have always wondered why Mark jumped. It isn't characteristic. He was a follower, not a leader.' She paused, wiping her eyes with the coloured scarf. Then she put her face into the scarf and sobbed. When she could speak, she said, 'I think he was so upset about what you did that he didn't care about himself. I can't forgive you for anything, of course, but what I hate you most for is not looking for him and looking after him in the morning. Or putting your head through the door of the tent to see if he was all right in the night. Except, I suppose, better that you didn't, because if you had put anything through the door of the tent, it would have been your disgusting willy.'

Roger was distracted from the force of this rebuke by embarrassment, for Betty's voice had risen, and people were noticing. She realised this herself, and became quiet.

'Now you know everything,' Roger dared to say.

'If I find I've got gaps, I'll come back,' said Betty, grimly. 'Had anything happened with you and Mark, before?'

'No.'

'Nothing?'

'Nothing. Except that I was in love with him, so I suppose my face lit up whenever I saw him.'

'So how could you do this to him?'

Betty did not expect an answer to this impossible question, and she did not get one. A few tears rolled down Roger's cheeks. 'You do know, don't you,' he said, 'that I'd do anything, anything at all, to have make that not have happened.'

'Yes, of course,' said Betty. It was not only that his feelings did not interest her. She loathed all of them.

'Did you know I was a clerical abuser, when you got in touch?' Roger asked.

'Yes. It was in the paper.'

'Did you think . . .?'

'Of course it came into my mind, but no one else seemed to think you had abused at St Malachy's, and the victim who denounced you was a good few years older than Mark, not a child.'

'Yes.' Utterly humiliated though he was already, Roger felt an extra pang to imagine the St Malachy mothers, to whom he had been a hero, interrogating their memories together, and, presumably, their sons' memories. 'I didn't love him as much as I loved Mark.'

'Love? You don't know the meaning of the word.'

'No, I suppose not.' Now Roger nerved himself to ask another question. 'Do you think you will go to the police?'

It was tempting to torture him with uncertainty, but the temptation waned. 'Well,' she said, 'why would I? Revenge won't bring him back, and I shall certainly never get so-called closure, whatever I do or don't do. So, no. You serve out your prison sentence, and take it for the two of them, and for any more secrets you may have. When you get out, your name will be on the sex offenders' list, so your life will be a misery anyway. So, no.'

Somehow Roger knew not to thank her. He sat and stared at the table. He hoped it would soon be four o'clock, but did not dare look at his watch.

'If Jack was alive, he would kill you,' Betty said again, looking at the thin, dejected figure hunched up on the other side of the table. This was how she would remember him, a poor, mean thing, who had wreaked disproportionate, unimaginable harm.

~

When the siren went for four o'clock, and Betty left, Roger immediately looked rather better. As he watched her recede into the crowd, he seemed to increase in size, not just because he was standing. He had wanted to shake her hand, but knew there was no hope of it. He was suffering in all sorts of ways; but at the same time he was steadied by having done what he had hoped to do: the right thing, and the brave thing. He thanked God for that grace. Gradually a certain relief began to make itself felt among his jumble of emotions, relief that at last, after twenty-two years, his crime had come home to the only person in the world who could mind it completely. In that sense, Mark had justice. She had been right, he thought, when she said he did not know what love is. But now that Mark was not his guilty secret, he might move towards minding about him in a new way. He did not know. He knew his heart was dry and narrow, and he knew that the only time in his life he had been shaken to the core by human beauty, he had ruined it. It was a lot to live with.

~

Betty struggled home on the train, taking wrong turnings on platforms, not sure what she was doing with her ticket. She took a taxi from Victoria. At home, she found Julia, with a tape measure and a friend, and pleaded illness. She closed her bedroom door and sat down on her bed.

She had much to think about, but was not ready to think, until the waves of raw pain had had their way. The train journey had interrupted their passage, and now they could come freely. They came. She could not be with Mark in the last eight or nine hours of his life, as she wanted to be. That was impossible. She suffered alone, as had he.

After half an hour, Julia came in with a cup of tea.

'Mum, you look awful,' she said. 'Go to bed. You are chilled. I'll get you a hot water bottle.'

Betty got into bed. She would have preferred to be in her warm sitting room, but in the circumstances, bed was the best option, the only place to be alone. She accepted the hot water bottle, and told Julia she would be fine in the morning, and no, she did not want anything to eat, and did not need to take her temperature.

She had moved from the huge category of mothers whose children die suddenly in horrible accidents, to the huge, though less huge, category of mothers whose children's last hours are spent in the hands of abusers. She was dwelling on, rather than coherently thinking about, what she had learned, and what Jack could never know. Jack had faced one kind of tragedy, as had she. He had never faced this one. In one sense she was glad that he had not. She did not know what it would have done to him. But twenty-two years ago, in the anguish of what they were facing then, he was beside her, minding as much as she did; and now she missed him terribly. But whilst there was a sigh of relief that Jack did not know, she knew she did not wish for ignorance, on her own behalf. Not to the slightest degree. It was too late to do anything to help or comfort Mark, but she could know. She could know.

She could know. But she could not talk. Without Jack, there was no one to talk to. She did not want to talk to Julia, because Julia's head was full of other things. Julia would not mind enough. She would be intrigued. She would have a theory. She would be sympathetic. Betty could not be bothered with any of that. There would be no solace for Betty in telling Julia. Further, Betty had told Roger she would not go to the police. Were Julia to be told, she probably would go to the police, which Betty did not want. Hatred, contempt and fury had their part in Betty's feelings, but revenge did not.

She saw Mark's face. It was an exceptionally lovely little face, and she saw it as it might have been when he was confused by abuse, and then, the next morning, by unfriendliness. He often had a sensitive, watchful expression, in which there was a hint of a smile; or that expression could come without the hint of a smile, and this is how Betty was seeing it now. He had suffered so little, under her care and Jack's. But she had seen that expression on his face when his hamster had died, when Reepicheep had set forth for the utter East, when he had found her in tears about her mother's death. Now she turned out the light, in case Julia came in again, and cried and cried.

Julia looked in before she left, and Betty pretended to be asleep. She heard Julia stealthily withdraw, saying, 'She's asleep. She's tired and chilled. She does this sometimes. She'll be fine.' Betty dozed and woke and dozed again, and got up at five o'clock. She made coffee. With her cold hands around the cup, she went to Mark's room, all ladders and pots of paint. She did not find Mark there. She did not need to.

Perhaps she was wrong, to decide against telling Julia. As Mark's sister, perhaps she should know. She believed Jack would think that. That would happen when it happened. Then, whether Julia went to the police or not would be her own decision. Jack would certainly have gone to the police.

Betty came downstairs again, sipping her coffee. She let herself out of the back door into her cold garden. She went to the bush where she and Jack and Julia and a few friends had scattered Mark's ashes. His ashes had long since become part of the soil, and the bush flourished. There is nothing you can do except suffer, she thought. Then she came indoors to face the day.

THE END

Bernardine Bishop on Writing

There is a fifty-year gap between my first two novels, published precociously in my early twenties, and my third, *Unexpected Lessons in Love*. In between I married, had my children, divorced, trained as a teacher, retrained as a psychotherapist, lost my parents, lost my sister, welcomed my sons' partners into our family, had grandchildren, married again and got cancer. Never once, during those fifty years, did it occur to me that I might write fiction again.

The day after I was told that my cancer had gone, I sat down and began this book. It was as if I had taken my life back and it was up to me to do something different with it. I had not known until then that I was longing to write, but even after fifty years I recognised the feeling.

After the first chapter, I fell in love with what I was writing. I remember thinking 'this is easy'; I remember the excitement, the energy that seemed to have been waiting there for me to tap into. I remember the delight at being in control of my own story again. During my treatment for cancer, the endless hospital appointments, the chemo and radiotherapy sessions, the agony of waiting for results, of sitting in front of doctors who knew more than I did about my future, I ceded authority to others. Now at my desk, I took it back. Cancer was one journey; my book would be another.

And once I had finished *Unexpected Lessons in Love* I could not stop. Since childhood, words and stories have been my natural habitat. I would not describe my need to write as a compulsion exactly, but I am conscious of enjoying it more than anything else I have done, of feeling entirely confident in what I was doing. I began my next book almost straight away. If *Unexpected Lessons* draws on my preoccupation with cancer and my longing for recovery, on the love I feel for my sons, and on my experiences of mothering, then *Hidden Knowledge* draws on my experiences as a therapist. A darker novel, it explores the things people do not know about themselves, the things they cannot face.

And after *Hidden Knowledge*, I went straight on to *The Street*. It is my final novel, because when I finished it I thought: this is it. I have shot my bolt. And I was right because the oncologist was wrong: the cancer has returned. It seems that it never went away. I wish tremendously strongly that I could write another book, but I know I have no more stories in me; I am too handicapped by illness. It may also be that I have told the stories I have to tell because *The Street* – a story of friendship, of longing, of people coming together – ends with the good death of an old man. As I wrote the last words and shut down the computer, I thought: this is enough. I have finished.

Bernardine Bishop – A Biography

Bernardine Bishop was born in London in 1939, just two months before the outbreak of the Second World War. The great-granddaughter of the poet Alice Meynell, Bernardine, along with her elder sister Gabriel, spent her earliest years with her grandmother, Madeleine, at the home Alice and Wilfred Meynell created for their family and its descendants at Greatham in West Sussex. Greatham remains a place of great importance to Bernardine and her family.

Bernardine Bishop's parents, Bernard and Barbara Wall, among the leading Catholic intellectuals of their day, were in Rome when war broke out, remaining there until 1940. Her mother, under her maiden name of Barbara Lucas, went on to write eight novels and also worked as a journalist for the *Observer* and the *Spectator* and as a translator. Her father was a distinguished historian of the Catholic Church and worked for British Intelligence during the war.

On returning to England, Barbara Wall became a land girl on a farm in Oxfordshire and took her daughters to live with her there. The sudden wrench away from Greatham and her beloved grandmother caused Bernardine great unhappiness. Returning to London after the war, Bernardine was educated at various Catholic schools, eventually gaining a place to read English Literature at Newnham College, Cambridge. This was the era when dons like F. R. Leavis and C. S. Lewis held sway in the lecture theatres and seminar rooms. Among Bernardine's contemporaries were David Frost and Peter Cook, and her lifelong friend, the novelist Margaret Drabble.

In 1960, on leaving Cambridge, Bernardine Bishop was co-opted as the youngest witness in the *Lady Chatterley* trial. She went on to write two early novels, worked as a reviewer and journalist and in 1961 married the pianist Stephen Bishop (now Stephen Kovacevich), who had come to London to study under Dame Myra Hess. Their elder son, Matt, was born in 1962; their younger, Francis, in 1964. By 1965 Bernardine and Stephen Bishop had separated and their marriage was eventually annulled.

To support herself and her young sons, Bernardine Bishop turned to teaching, eventually becoming Head of English at a London comprehensive school. She then went on to have a distinguished career as a psychotherapist, training at the London Centre for Psychotherapy and also working as a tutor and supervisor. She co-wrote a number of books on psychotherapy and contributed to many academic and professional journals. Cancer forced her retirement in 2010 and she returned to her first love, fiction. Of the three novels she wrote during this period, the first, *Unexpected Lessons in Love*, was published in January 2013. *Hidden Knowledge* is the second and it was followed by *The Street*. Until her death in July 2013, Bernardine Bishop lived in London with her husband, Bill Chambers, whom she married in 1981.

The Street

*an extract from Bernardine Bishop's forthcoming book,
soon to be available from Sceptre*

Bernardine Bishop

Chapter 1

Sometimes it is impossible to turn even a short London street into a village. But sometimes it can be easily done. It all depends on one or two personalities.

Palmerston Street was a short street. But even at that it had twenty-eight front doors, fourteen even numbers on one side and fourteen odd numbers on the other. Each side was a row of Victorian cottages. Long since, they had all been built on to at the back, offering an extra room or two, to the shrinkage of the small gardens. Some had lofts added; others, less satisfactorily because of the proximity of an underground river, had cellars rendered habitable. Some had both.

Palmerston Street was less of a village than some residents would have liked it to be, but more so than suited others. The majority of the households will not come into this story. The people who lived in the houses that will not figure had been urban for generations, did not think in terms of neighbours and neighbourhoods, but got on with busy lives in other places and circles, or in houses that changed hands often, and never settled down in long ownership. Most households noticed and had an attitude to the village spirit in the street, either welcoming it, feeling intrigued and embraced, or hating the notion that strangers might know their business and that there might be the twitch of a lace curtain. Such divisions could exist even within a household.

Anne Darwin was a retired property surveyor in her late sixties. Those of the street who took note of its atmosphere thought Anne was at the centre of what made the street a community. Community was Anne's word, and some people liked it and others did not. Anne had a history of making communities out of collections of people, be they streets, offices or parents at the schools her daughter attended. To some she was a treasure, to others, a pain.

In good weather she would often stand outside her house for half an hour in the afternoon, her dark cardigan stretched double by crossed arms, her thin figure full of expectation, her eyes darting up and down the street. Lonely people, gossipy people, people with little children, people who were her friends, would stop and talk to her. She was the grapevine. If a house in the street was for sale, she was the person to come to for the low-down. Some conversations were fleeting, others long. Sometimes several neighbours simultaneously would stop in their tracks and collect around her.

Her husband, Eric, did not share her interest, nor approve of her enthusiasm. When she stood at their gate, he would some-times look out of the front window at her eager, lithe back view. He hid behind the curtain and peered, in case she looked round, and in case his curiosity was spotted by one of her prey. As far as he knew, he was struggling with uncomfortable emotions of contempt and embarrassment. But he also felt the pain of exclusion. Anne was surviving retirement, in a way he was not being able to. She had found a new interest. It was a pathetic interest, but Eric had not found an interest at all.

When he learned that he and Anne were to have a grandson staying with them, he had a sinking feeling that Anne hoped this would be an interest for him, and that it would not be. Their daughter and husband had to be in Canada for a year, and had decided to leave John in London with his grandparents to start the good secondary school in which they had secured him a place. The two younger children were to go to Canada with their parents. So there were two new things in Eric's life – retirement; and the approaching advent of John, aged eleven.

The four adults involved had not seriously wondered whether John would be all right. The parents were stimulated and pre-occupied by the prospect of their year abroad. John would come to Canada and join them for the Christmas holiday. They put it to John that September to December is not very long. It was exciting for John, they told each other, to be starting big school, and lucky that the school was walking distance from Palmerston Street. Everything, from their point of view, was falling into place. On her part, Anne's mind had turned immediately to rooms and spaces within her house. John could have the attic, which surely a child would like. Anne liked a challenge, and was prepared to throw herself into this one; but it occurred to her to wish that she knew John better. The young family had lived in Edinburgh and Manchester so far, which hadn't favoured easy meetings with the children's maternal ancestry. Anne had been known to wonder, disloyally, why John was not to be boarded with his other grand-parents who, as they lived in Edinburgh, John must at least at one time have seen more of. But it was to be London for Clifford and Sara after Toronto, so they were establishing John in London, which made perfect sense.

Eric alone gave way to a qualm, and said to Anne, 'Won't John miss his family?' To which Anne, who thought Eric was trying to get out of it, answered breezily, 'We are his family.'

It was still August, so there was a fortnight's grace before John's arrival. Late August in the street saw inhabitants returning from holidays. There was unpacking of cars, there were shouted greetings and welcoming waves. Window boxes had been faith-fully watered, cats fed, and those who had discharged these obligations breathed small sighs of relief. Anne stood at her front gate; Eric watched unwillingly from within.

Eric was a hoarder, or so Anne thought. One of the effects of this characteristic was that he still had his boyhood books. In this fortnight he took to climbing to and from the attic, furnishing what would be John's quarters with appropriate classics. Anne liked to hear his heavy tread up and down the ladder, proving that he was taking an interest and, in his own way, providing for John.

Sometimes she stopped whatever she was doing and listened, just to hear him.

'It's a bit hot up there,' Eric said to Anne. He was a big man and his broad forehead was sweating.

'Have you opened the skylights?'

'No. I thought pigeons might come in.'

'Pigeons?'

'There's pigeon shit on the skylight glass.'

Taken aback, Anne considered. Eventually she said, 'When the room's inhabited, they won't want to come in.'

Eric didn't answer, and was having a drink of water. 'Hot work,' he said.

～

Later, Anne went up to the attic, her feet brisker and less creaky on the narrow steps than Eric's. She wished she knew whether John was the kind of person who had to pee in the night. She did not like the idea of his coming up and down the ladder half asleep. She had put an elegant red plastic bucket in an obscure corner of the attic, but she knew it would be difficult for her to put into words to John what it was potentially for.

A mild thrill of excitement ran through her whenever she saw the attic. It was the kind of excitement that goes straight back to childhood. The attic was so big, so quiet, so bare and so neat. It had its own smell – slightly musty and outhousey, but pleasant. An adult could stand at full height only in the middle; it would be easier for John. There were the two skylights, and when, as now, it was sunny, they threw geometrical shapes of yellow on to the floor. There was a chest of drawers, a desk, a chair for the desk, a radiator and a bookcase. There was a futon, on which Anne had arranged pretty, patterned bedding. With its minimal furniture, well spread out, the attic appeared sparse, almost monastic and was spacious, for it spanned the whole length and breadth of the house. Eric had said if they were doing anything up there they might as well have a full loft conversion, and make a proper room of it, or two, improving the value of the house. Anne had wanted a much less ambitious job, keeping the contours of the roof and putting in little more than insulation, a floor and a ceiling. Then there had been the skylights and the electricity. Finally the blue fitted carpet, which made the space look even bigger. People did not often sleep up here, as the Darwins had a spare bedroom. But Anne loved the idea that the attic was there, and now she was pleased that it would come into its own for John.

Bending her head when necessary, and finally walking with a crouch, Anne studied the books Eric had been putting on the shelves. Stevenson – *Treasure Island*, *The Black Arrow*, *Kidnapped* and some poems. A long row of faded, hardback Hornblowers. Five or six *Swallows and Amazons*. *King Solomon's Mines*. *The Jungle Book*. Several Biggles. Anne was touched by Eric's choices. She knew she might have been confronted by the spines of *Ivanhoe* and *Beowulf*, favourites which happily seemed to have been rejected, and must still be reposing on Eric's own shelves. She could, if Eric's judgement had failed him completely, have been offended by the title of *Lorna Doone*. Or *Kim*.

Now she looked at the desk, scribbled on, wooden and steady, Sara's desk actually. Perhaps she could tell John that. The surface was big enough for a laptop, without the laptop having to take up all the space, and there were four drawers which Anne now checked were empty. Immediately above the desk was the trap door to the roof, renewed by the loft men, and tidily bolted. Beside that was a smoke alarm. All seemed in order.

Anne opened one of the skylights. Her head popped out into warm, bright air. The white clouds seemed very near. It was odd, and nice, not to be able to see downwards, but only upwards. There could be no checking whether a neighbour was going by. She could hear pigeons, but could not see them, and the purring noise was soothing. She decided to leave the skylight open for the moment, but would have to remember to come up to close it if there was a threat of rain.

Because she was so high and so sequestered, she did not hear the doorbell, and by the time she was downstairs, Eric had gone to the door, and was in conversation with Georgia Fox. Georgia saw Anne appear behind Eric, and called, 'Oh, Anne.'

Anne pushed forward. 'Has something happened?'

'Brenda has been taken to hospital. Didn't you see the ambulance?'

'No. What's happened?

'I don't know. It was all incredibly quick. Five minutes ago. I heard the ambulance, it stopped outside Brenda's, I was still wondering what was happening and whether to go over, when a stretcher came out, then off they went. Didn't you hear the ambulance?'

'No. Come in, Georgia.'

It was worrying for both of them not to understand something that had happened in the street and Anne made tea. Eric withdrew, not as incurious as he hoped to seem. Anne and Georgia sat in Anne's kitchen, each with a frown of concern on her face. Georgia's house was opposite Brenda's at the other end of the street, and it was Georgia who had the key to Brenda's house.

'Has she seemed unwell?' Anne asked.

'Not really,' said Georgia, hoping she had not been negligent. 'I know I went in yesterday morning, and we did the crossword. Brenda was still in bed, but she always is, until her carers come. Oh dear, I wish I had gone in this morning.' She paused. 'I'd better go in now. No one will have fed the cat.'

'I'll come with you.' Together they hurried up the street. Anne was energised by a crisis which did not affect her emotions, for she did not know Brenda well. Georgia loved Brenda, and was puzzled about how to get news of her. She did not even know which hospital she had gone to.

When Georgia let them in to Brenda's house, two carers, known to Georgia, in bright blue uniforms, were sitting in the kitchen, making notes and phone calls.

'It must be you who called the ambulance,' said Georgia. 'Which hospital has she gone to?'

The carers confirmed this and gave the name of the hospital. 'We've fed Ben,' said one of them, seeing Georgia look round for the cat. In fact Benn had two 'n's to his name, for he was called after Tony Benn. He would have been called Tony, but for Tony Blair.

The story came out. The carers had arrived and let themselves in as usual. They had called out as usual but, unusually, there was no answering cry. The senior carer's fingers had been on her mobile almost as they entered Brenda's bedroom. 'I thought she had passed away.'

'And had she?'

'We thought so, and so did the paramedics, but they took her, anyway, because that's routine. If there's a chance.'

'We'll miss her,' said the smaller carer, who had not spoken yet.

'She wouldn't want to be resuscitated,' said Georgia, quietly crying.

Brenda Byfleet, who had lived in the street for decades, and living in the street had gone from the briskness of early middle age to a housebound ninety, was not famous. But Georgia Fox had heard of her, and been thrilled to discover, ten years ago, that Brenda lived in a house opposite the one she was buying. Georgia was a generation younger than Brenda. When Georgia became involved in peace projects, Brenda Byfleet was a name in that small world. Brenda had not missed a step of any of the Aldermaston marches. She had lived for three years on Greenham Common. She had chained herself to railings. She had been in prison. She had distributed leaflets and organised petitions. In old age she had marched, or limped, against the attacks on Afghanistan and Iraq. On the terrible evening when she realised that this last, enormous march had cut no ice with the government, she sat and cried. 'We have achieved nothing,' she said to Georgia.

In a curious way, inconspicuous to both, by the time of Brenda's death, each of these two women had become the most important person in the other's life. It should be said that people were not very important to either, in an intimate sense; so the competition was not severe. Brenda's lifelong singleness arose, at least in part, from her singleness of purpose. She had family money from tea plantations, which income source worried her terribly; but on the other hand, it was convenient not to have to earn. She balanced the good she hoped she did against the exploitative nature of her daily bread.

For unmarried women of Brenda's generation, to be a virgin was not seriously eccentric. No one marvelled at it in Brenda's case, for she was neither beautiful nor charming, nor had she ever thought to try to be. She was direct, loud-voiced, opinionated and well-informed. She was energetic and stout, with unkempt hair, and she never gave clothes a thought, unless she had to speak publicly or go to a do or a funeral, which occasions made her stare helplessly at her clothes until friends assembled a uniform for her. Women and men were her friends indiscriminately, and if there were no common causes, the friendships failed unnoticed. Her warmth and her laugh attracted people to her, her command of current facts, and her courage.

And now she was dead. Georgia phoned the hospital, and heard the news. She put the receiver down, and stared out of the window. Brenda's house looked the same as always, and poor Benn was sitting on the doorstep, washing a paw. Georgia's own doorbell rang. It was Anne.

'You must be upset,' she said to Georgia.

'I can't believe it,' Georgia said. 'That's the main feeling.'

Together they looked at Brenda's house. Finally Georgia said, 'What about the cat?'

'I'll have him,' said Anne, who always liked stepping in. She hoped she would not regret it. Might a cat be an interest for Eric? And nice for John?

Nieces, never seen before, came to Brenda's house. It was Anne who found out that they were nieces, and that when they had cleared the house, they planned to sell it. Georgia and Anne went to Brenda's cremation, organised by the nieces, quick and disappointing. On the evening of the cremation, Georgia took a key and, rather furtively, crossed the road to Brenda's house. She wanted to say some sort of goodbye. It was Brenda's small and untidy study that she particularly wanted to see, and be in, for the last time. It had a cluttered desk, no curtains, and photos pinned to the walls. There was a special smell, and there was the battered armchair in which Georgia had been sitting when Brenda said, 'We have achieved nothing,' and cried, with those terrible hoarse sobs. Georgia was nervous, for her visit was illicit, and her existence not known to the nieces. She turned the key in the lock as so often before, but the door resisted utterly. She pushed. Then she realised the nieces had deadlocked the door, as well they might. Georgia's latchkey made it do no more than shift a millimetre. Brenda never used the deadlock, and Georgia had not imagined there was one, nor noticed its disused keyhole. Such a thing was inimical to Brenda. Georgia hurried home. The house was alien territory now, and Georgia relinquished any claim to it.

Georgia and Anne had not been real friends until now. They were both people who liked the street to be a street or, as some would say, the street to be a soap; and that had always been a link. But they were no more than warm acquaintances. Anne did not even know what Georgia did for a living. But Brenda's death brought them together. Together they walked down the street rattling a carton of cat biscuits, calling and mewing, to lure Benn to his new home. This project involved a number of expeditions, for Benn would eat the offered cat biscuit in Anne's kitchen, but then jump out of the window to make his way back to outside Brenda's locked front door. Other neighbours took food to him there, which did not help. Anne and Georgia found licked plates on Brenda's doorstep. Then Anne managed to put it about that she was taking Benn, and the project of Benn's house-move became a street project. Meanwhile Eric was working on a cat flap in his back door.

'I don't even know what you do,' said Anne to Georgia, when they had despairingly watched Benn's muscular tabby hindquarters disappear out of the window yet again. 'Is he ever going to feel at home here?'

'Give him time,' said Georgia. 'Well, I'm a zoologist.'

'Zoologist? What sort? Academic?'

'Yes.' Georgia mentioned where she worked.

'Well.' Anne was strangely pleased.

'Gastropods,' said Georgia, encouraged by the expression on Anne's face. 'Molluscs. Snails, really.'

'Snails!' said Anne, only ever having thought of them as a garden pest. 'Snails. Eric wages war on them in the garden.'

'I wish he wouldn't. And everyone does. The garden snail is fast becoming an endangered species.'

~

After three or four more days Benn was able to sit and wash on a chair in Anne's kitchen, rather than making a dash for it the minute he had eaten. Eric and Anne both felt proud to see him there. He had accepted them. The next day he worked Eric's cat flap, and Eric felt honoured. Georgia wondered what had happened in Benn's mind to enable him to make the transition. She did not like to think it had been easy.

'I suppose Brenda will be forgotten,' she said sadly to Eric and Anne.

'Won't she have an obituary?' said Anne.

'She hasn't had one in the *Independent*,' said Eric.

'Nor in the *Guardian*,' said Georgia.

They were silent.

'She didn't have any children, that's the problem,' said Anne, then could have bitten her tongue, for Georgia didn't either.

But luckily Georgia didn't seem to be listening. After half a minute she looked up, and said, 'So when it comes down to it, what is a life?'

'What do you mean, what is a life?' said Eric. 'Here we are, we are born, we live, we die, some of us after shorter lives, some longer.'

'But all Brenda's thoughts, passions, letters to prime ministers,

letters to . . . All her direct action, conversations, hopes. Memories
– yes, memories! – going back to the peace movement before the
war, the thirties – all that, leave alone her personal life . . . All
gone.'

'She should have written a book,' said Anne. Georgia felt that
people always say this, as a way of avoiding the question: what
is a life?

~

When Georgia got home, happy and not happy that there was
no Benn sitting patiently on Brenda's doorstep, she started
wondering whether to put together an 'Other Lives' on Brenda
for the *Guardian*. She was baulked by the lack of solid information. She had only known Brenda for the last decade of
Brenda's nine, and they had no mutual friends. The impulse faded.

But the impact of Brenda's death did not fade. Georgia had
just started a sabbatical year, her last, as within the next seven
years she would retire. She had been looking forward to her
sabbatical, and thought she was full of research interests. In
November she was going to join a project studying the special
qualities of the shells of desert snails in the Sinai. It had been
very exciting to be invited on this prestigious enterprise. She had
intended to do a lot of work beforehand, starting now. But because
of Brenda, the heart had gone out of it.

It was not only that she missed Brenda, nor that a close death
brings all death closer. She was also struggling with a sense of the
vanity of human endeavour. Seventy years, at a guess, of aspiration,
resilience, toil and dedication; and what was there to show for
Brenda? What was there to show for what she had striven for?
And yet, what else is there to do in a life, but try to make things
better? Or, in Georgia's own case, to add a tiny bit to what we
know about snails?

Join a literary community of
like-minded readers who seek out
the best in contemporary writing.

From the thousands of submissions Sceptre
receives each year, our editors select the books
we consider to be outstanding.

We look for distinctive voices, thought-provoking
themes, original ideas, absorbing narratives and
writing of prize-winning quality.

If you want to be the first to hear about our
new discoveries, and would like the chance to
receive advance reading copies of our books
before they are published, visit

www.sceptrebooks.co.uk

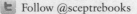 Follow @sceptrebooks

 'Like' SceptreBooks

Watch SceptreBooks